The Forgotten Tales Of

El Capitán

The Forgotten Tales Of

El Capitán

By Alex Negrón

Self-Published with assistance from
MIDNIGHT EXPRESS BOOKS

The Forgotten Tales Of El Capitán

Self-Published with assistance from

MIDNIGHT EXPRESS BOOKS
POBox 69
Berryville AR 72616
MEBooks1@yahoo.com

The Forgotten Tales Of

El Capitán

By Alex Negrón

Acknowledgements

I would like to thank my Eternal and thrice Holy God for this precious gift given to me. May He get the praise for saving my wretched soul and everything I do successfully. I would like to also thank my mother, Carmen, her unconditional love and motherly patience has shaped me to become the man I am today, I love you lady!

I want to thank all my mentors from DePaul University, Northeastern University and Chicago Theological Seminary as well as North Park University. Continue to do the great work you do to chip away at these walls of Jericho - you know who you are.

I want to thank my father and everyone who supported, inspired and pushed me to be great. Thank you so much, I can't name you all, but just know that each of you are stored in my corazón para siempre.

Lastly, I want to thank some of my friends; Pepe, Ana and Manny. May God continue to bless you and your beautiful children. It is a blessing to call you my family.

This book would not be possible without any of you - Thank you so much.

Sincerely,

Alex

Viva El Capitán!

Contents

Matters of the Heart

Welcome to the adventurous world of the Seven Seas. I ask that you join me and have a seat. Please enjoy this wonderful tale that they dare me to never speak. It's about a man who was erased from the history of Spain and charged with treason against his native land. But these bitter waters, revere him as a brave and loyal man. Beyond these pages are the forgotten tales of el Capitán and his rebel band...

El Capitán was born in the town of Seville on a cold winter day in the year of 1684. Being the son of the town's Butcher, Alejandro De Los Amantes could not picture himself inheriting the family trade, so he ended up finding his way into Spain's Naval Fleet at the age of fifteen. At a very early age, Alejandro became enamored with the wild stories that fishermen boasted while they sold their merchandise in the market square. His imagination would carry him to the new world that Spain proudly claimed as its own.

Now Alejandro and his men are on board the "Amante Del Mar" and are surrounded by the evil Admiral Rodriguez and his ferocious fleet. His men are scurrying back and forth, trying to survive the aggressive assault by their enemy. Alejandro's heart-rate is slowing down as he looks left and right to find a solution. He glances at his enemy's face and sees a look of much awaited content. He hears a demonic chuckle from the Admiral while he signals the go ahead to fire the cannons.

In the midst of the cannons blasting and roaring, and his crew going into a chaotic panic, he sees a pretty woman standing in front of his quarters.

"Catalina?" he asks in a confused state.

The ship rips and shreds as it takes on the heavy artillery. He tries his best to get to Catalina, but the ship can no longer hold on to its integrity.

"Catalina!" he exclaims as he tries to reach out for her one last time.

"Capitán," someone yells out as he shakes under the water.

"Capitán!"

His eyes open up while he regains his breath. It's just a dream. His oldest friend is standing on the side of his bed with a worried look on his face.

"Capitán, are you ok? "

"Yes," he replies as he takes a deep breath to calm himself down, "It was just a bad sueño, Guillermo."

Guillermo shakes his head as he asks, "Was it a sueño of Admiral Rodriguez?"

Guillermo is the one who introduced El Capitán to the sailing world. He met the young Alejandro while saving him from a group of men who worked for a royal dignitary that was getting the best of him near the town pier. He is the oldest member of El Capitán's ship at the age fifty. He's also the most skilled of the bunch, and if you let him tell it, he's seen all that the seas can offer. He loves to tell tales of the adventures that he has survived while serving his beloved España, but no one believes his stories. The only one who does is El Capitán and he does so because it adds fuel to his childhood imagination. Guillermo gets excited every time he orates the mysterious tales of the Kraken, Fountain of Youth, and the Secret Order of the True Protectors of the Seven Seas. The rest of the crew shrugs him off and ridicule him to get him to shut up.

"Yes," El Capitán replies, "but this sueño is very different."

"How is it so?"

"This felt real and there was a woman on board the ship."

"What woman," Guillermo asks to help him make sense of the dream.

"Catalina," he says as he sits up to get out of his bed.

"Cata..." Guillermo says as he scratches his temple, "is that the señorita that you fell in love with when you were a child?"

"Si," he replies with a look that tells Guillermo that he does not want to speak any more about it.

"Capitàn…"

"Forget it, Guillermo, what are you doing in my cabin?"

"We are going to land on shore soon and the prisoner wishes to speak to you.''

"I'll speak to that criminal when we arrive. Now go, get the men ready to dock the ship."

"Si, Capitàn," he says as he walks away in a hurried fashion.

"And Guillermo…"

"Si, Capitàn?"

"Viva El Mar!"

"Viva El Mar," he replies as he salutes his Captain.

Alejandro gets himself together before he steps out of his cabin. He takes a look in the mirror and is satisfied with the results. He is a very handsome man with flowing locks of dark hair that draws out his Emerald green eyes and chiseled chin. He has the stance of a prize-winning thorough-bred from the land of Arabia. All the women who cross his path, have a deep yearning to obtain his love, but his heart cannot be possessed because the Seven Seas claims it, and the Seven Seas is in España's possession.

El Capitàn is a man of honor, integrity and trustworthiness. The men on his ship do just as he commands and they do it with joy. There have been rumors in the territories of España that they are more loyal to him than to the Monarch they serve.

He steps out of his cabin and sees his men doing their tasks as the ship leans closer to home.

"Captain on deck," exclaims his second-in-command, Javier Lopez.

"At ease," El Capitàn says to relieve each man of their honorable salute.

A majority of El Capitàn's men owe their lives to him and they serve him loyally until their final breath leaves their souls. They come from different walks and paths of life, but they share the common goal of a united brotherhood, regardless of color, creed, or race.

"We are approaching shore, Captain," Javier says.

"Guillermo gave me the status, XO."

Javier has been by El Capitán's side for eight years. They met while El Capitán was on leave while serving Admiral Rodriguez's ship. El Capitán stopped by a very seedy watering hole named "El Ojo Negro". That happened to be the very same day that Javier's con-artist ways came back to bite him in the back of his behind.

Javier had deceived a wealthy aristocrat into believing that he was purchasing some very authentic Italian paintings that date back to the beginning of the Renaissance period. The aristocrat paid Javier a small fortune, and three months later, three hired men found him in the bar. All the money had been wasted away from gambling, partying and paying back the debt he owed the barrio loan shark, El Gordo.

Javier's ruggedly-handsome looks are the key to his rakish demeanor. His up-to-date apparel to match his long hair, and also the way he speaks, makes people feel at ease around him and believe that he's speaking the truth. His eloquent speech is like a soothing stream and his manly stature at six foot-one is very inviting and receptive. Javier's every move was a game to him and every bit of it thrilled him. The thrill from playing these conniving games was the only thing that got him up in the morning. On that day in "El Ojo Negro", that game was no longer a thrill, it got very real, very fast.

Something about Javier's demeanor intrigued Alejandro and it made his life worth saving. Granted, it was none of Alejandro's business, but his intrigue caused him to step in and help the Caballero in distress. He fought by Javier's side and helped him escape the Aristocrat's goons and leave the tavern unscathed. Javier joined the Navy and he vowed to never leave his new companion's side as long as he lived. After several years of traveling the seas with Alejandro, he learned how to have a conscience and decided to right all the wrongs whenever the chance presented itself. He even paid the aristocrat the debt he owed.

Every now and then, while on stays from their long journeys, Javier receives a slap or two from the women he's wronged in the past. El Capitán welcomes those times with supreme joy because it helps keep Javier in a state of humility.

Alejandro stands next to his pilot, Rogelio the Moor, as he scans the horizon with his periscope. He nudges his seasoned pilot and cracks a smile.

"Land up ahead, my Moorish friend. Be careful this time, Rogelio."

"Si, Capitán," he replies as he smiles back.

His name is not really Rogelio, but Guillermo found it hard to pronounce his Islamic name and dubbed him "El Mauricio Rogelio". It did not bother him one bit. Especially after being pulled out of the freezing Atlantic. He was holding on to the plank of a damaged Slave Ship that was headed towards the Colonies of England four years ago.

"Otavio, Tuyen, and Pho." he yells to get their attention.

The three sailors make their way to El Capitán to receive their instructions.

"Si, Capitán," Otavio replies.

"Ready the prisoner to hand him over to the Harbor Master. I want you three to also handle restocking the ship with the supplies we need in case we must head out quickly."

"Si, Capitán, we'll see to it," Pho says.

Otavio is Alejandro's cousin through marriage. He is the youngest at the age of sixteen, and he is very eager to prove himself to be worthy of the name sailor. Tuyen and Pho are both called the Chinamen Twins, but no one knows why. Neither is from China, and they don't look alike, and no one knows if they are even related. I guess the name stuck with them after they got saved from a Moorish mob of angry traders in a market near Casa Blanca. The Chinamen Twins were originally silk traders and their cheap prices on expensive rugs made them targets for stoning until El Capitán and Javier stepped in on their behalf. They are very skilled in explosives and they are tasked with the maintenance of the ship's artillery. They let Otavio tag along as their apprentice.

Also along on the "Amante Del Mar" are Edwin, Crissino, Cristobal, Alberto, Pablo, and Eduardo. Together they forge a friendship and brotherhood that is stronger than the Atlantic winds during hurricane season.

Rogelio steers the ship towards the pier and guides it very carefully to the loading dock. El Capitán and his men are charged with the special task to bring back very exquisite treasures from the New World to the King and Queen of España. For decades, the kingdom has had a very large problem with thieving English pirates and El Capitán is quickly becoming the solution to that problem.

They are finally returning from a very arduous trip and each man cannot wait to step back on safe land.

Rogelio finally docks the ship, and the Chinamen Twins haul the prisoner from below the deck and bring him to El Capitán.

"Hold it right there," El Capitán says, "You may speak now before I turn you over to the Harbor Master's custody while you await trial."

"Please Capitán, I was forced to attack your ship, have mercy on my soul."

"It is not my duty to have mercy on loathsome criminals, it is the duty of El Señor up above, then His majesty; which you'll see muy pronto."

"Please, it was El Tiburón who—"

"Ayy." El Capitán says as he raises his hand, "Take him away."

"Please Signoné. I'm begging you, they will hang me!" the prisoner exclaims as Tuyen and Pho drag him away.

A huge chunky man is awaiting El Capitán as he steps off the ship. He's wearing the standard-issued naval uniform and he sports a thin moustache that disappears when he moves his lips. The plump cheeks and round stomach causes Alejandro to shake his head in wonder. He constantly asks himself, when did Harbor Master Gonzalez decide to let himself go?

"Buenos dias, Harbor Master," he says as he salutes him.

"Como estas, Capitán?"

"Estoy muy bien."

"So how's the ship?"

"Well, she's still floating, but the rudder is slightly damaged and the bottom deck need reinforcement," El Capitán replies.

"I'll have the shipmen get on it as soon as possible. You have been summoned to attend the Royal Palace. The Rey himself requests you, Capitán."

"Is that so?"

"Si, the Principe is getting engaged and you have been invited to attend. Perhaps, a much awaited promotion to command your own fleet."

El Capitán bursts out at the Harbor master's insinuation. After twenty seconds of sharing a laugh with him, he hands over his Captain's log so that the troubling journey can be recorded and stored in the Harbor Master's office.

"I lost four good men to attain this mythical map to reach the lost Incan city. I hope for the sake of Dios, their lives were worthy for my Lord's cause.

"I'm sure they were. I'll see that their families are compensated for their loss," the Harbor Master says as he makes the formation of the Cross to give the fallen their due respect.

"The gold is stored in the bottom deck chamber and you'll see the charges against the prisoner in my Captain's log."

"Very well, Capitán, Viva España."

"Viva España, Harbor master, Viva España."

"Capitán," Javier says.

"How can I help you amigo?"

"The men await your final orders."

"As of now, they are relieved of their sailing duties. They are to gather at the tavern to receive their wages and they will be on leave until we return."

"Return?" Javier asks confusedly, "Return from where?"

"We have been summoned by the King to attend his heir's engagement party."

Javier gives his commanding officer a proper salute and walks away to relay El Capitán's orders. El Capitán leaves in the opposite direction and walks towards the Harbor Master's office to retrieve the ship's wages from the assistant, Ramón.

"Hola Ramón," he says as he steps in, "Como estas mi amigo?"

"Bien, bien," he replies as he nods his head.

"How's your wife and all those kids?"

"They are fine as well. They have been counting the days for the return of their famous Uncle to tell them another one of your aventuras. So tell me, Capitán, when are you going to settle down and have children of your own?"

"Ha! Ha!" El Capitán says, "Oh no, no, Ramón! Mi Corazón belongs to el mar and her womb is barren!"

"Ha! Ha," Ramón says as he joins in on the joke. "You are very funny, Capitán!"

He hands him the bags of silver for he and his men's wages. Ramón is short and frail and unfit for the rigorous lifestyle of a Spanish Sailor. The droopiness of his eyes gives the very reserved man the appearance that he's afraid of his own shadow.

Every now and then Ramón invites Alejandro over for supper and has him tell his children some of the great adventures that the Atlantic has to offer.

"Are you stopping by for supper tonight?"

"I'm sorry Ramón, I have been summoned to the Royal palace. Please give Gloria my regards and let her know that I will gladly receive her gracious hospitality when I return. Tell the children that I will tell them the victory I gained near San Juan Bay over El Tiburón."

"El Tiburón?"

"Si, he's an evil pirate with an ugly face and the teeth of a Great White Tiburón."

"Wow! Capitán tell me more," Ramón says with interest.

"I can't right now, I'll tell you when I return from the palace."

" Okay, Capitán, may el mano de Dios continue to lead you."

"Same to you amigo."

El Capitán walks out of the office and he heads towards the friendly tavern "Naranjos" with the bags of silver on his shoulders. You can easily spot the tavern from the pier. Just above the entrance, there's a brightly painted sign of an orange hanging over it.

As he gets closer, he can hear the tavern's band playing and the normal ruckus that a tavern contains within its walls.

Most of the tavern's customers are both local fishermen and Spanish sailors on brief stays.

He enters the bar and immediately hears, "Hola Capitán!"

He graciously removes his hat to acknowledge their greeting as he weaves his way towards the back. Two fishermen playing cards get into an argument and exchange blows while he approaches them. He puts the bags of silver down and gets between them.

"What's going on?!" he exclaims.

"He's a cheater!" the one on the left says.

"I'll show you who's a cheater!" the other says as he tries to go through El Capitán.

"Stop! Come on Gilberto, let me see your sleeves."

"I am appalled Capitán!"

Capitán swoops from behind Gilberto and snatches his left wrist and grips it to put it behind his back. As soon as he does so, cards slide out his sleeve.

"What is this Gilberto?! You know Angel does not take well to cheaters in his tavern!"

"I know Capitán! It was an honest mistake! Ouch, you're hurting me!"

"The honest mistake." El Capitán calmly says as he applies more pressure to Gilberto's wrist "was leaving you off with a warning on your first offense! Come, get this piece of scum out of this tavern!"

Two men grab hold of him, and they roughly escort him out of the tavern while El Capitán straightens his uniform. He then walks over to the nicely cut-out section that is reserved for he and his men.

The tavern owner, Angel Pedro Pagán, makes sure that El Capitán always has a place in his tavern. Angel's stature towers over the entire crowd as he makes his way towards El Capitán to bring him his mug of Spanish Ale.

Angel is just three years removed from returning from the battlefield. He inherited the tavern from his seedless older brother, Julio, who passed away from an unknown illness. When Angel took over, the bar was being overrun by the local goons and El Capitán, along with Guillermo and Javier, helped Angel kick out the goons and clean the place up to make it a legitimate establishment. To show his gratitude, Angel reserves a special section for El Capitán and keeps the ales flowing when they return from the rugged seas.

"Here's our wages men," he says as he puts the bags on the wobbly table.

"To El Capitán!" exclaims Edwin as he puts his mug in the air.

"To El Capitán!" the entire tavern says out loud.

"No, no, no," El Capitán says as he tries to humbly silence their cheers, "to you, to all of you! Each of you are great men and worthy to be called Sailors of España!"

Angel finally gets to El Capitán with an obvious limp that he obtained from the war against the brutal English and El Capitán shaves off a stack of silver coins and hands it to Angel.

"Oh no, Capitán, your generosity is not required, I owe you more than you owe me."

"Please, take it Angel, you are a member of our crew." El Capitán raises his mug and says, "To Angel, the anchor to our souls! He gives us a place to call home."

"To Angel!" The tavern yells out loud as the band plays more music while the crowd gets back to having a good time.

"Gather around men," El Capitán says. "I have been requested to see the King. Your orders are to stay near, and see that the ship gets the proper care and be ready for our next mission."

Javier divides the salary evenly among each sailor. Although El Capitán has the right to attain a quarter of all the wages, he takes an equal share. In El Capitán's eyes, not one man is greater than another's, regardless of their rank.

El Capitán finishes his ale, tucks his wages in his pockets and he signals his second-in-command to finish his ale as well.

"I want to get to the Royal Palace at dawn, Javier."

"I will find us a coachman to get us there."

Javier walks out and gets to his task while El Capitán makes his rounds to greet everyone at the tavern before he leaves out. When he gets out, Javier is out front with a horse carriage ready to get them to their destination.

Alejandro takes a quick glance at the sky and he sees the Sun and Moon give each other a nod before the Sun departs towards the West. He steps up and enters the coach and gives himself a good stretch to go with a yawn.

"To the Royal palace," Javier says as he knocks on the front of the carriage.

The coachman rides throughout the night. The galloping horses provide a sound that causes Javier and Alejandro to take a much needed slumber. The Sun's rays peek through the window and catch the right eye of El Capitán and it causes him to slowly wake up. The horses ease up on their pace as they approach the guards at the Royal Palace's entrance.

"Señores, we are at your destination," the old man says.

The head of the palace guard opens the carriage door to inquire who the occupants are.

"Welcome to the Royal Palace. Please state the nature of your visit."

"My name is Alejandro De Los Amantes of His Majesty's Royal Navy. This is Javier Lopez, my Executive Officer, and we have been invited to attend the Prince's engagement ball."

"May I see your invitations, Capitán?"

El Capitán pulls out the invitations and hands them to the guard before he steps out of the carriage. Javier follows behind him and the coachman gives a look to find out who will pay him while the guard scans the authenticity of the invitations.

"Uhm, uhm," the coachman says.

"Oh, perdona me Señor, where are my manners?" El Capitán says,

"Guard, please pay the man for his troubles."

The guard looks up with a disgruntled look and says, "Very well, the King has arranged a chamber for the both of you." He goes in his pocket and gives the coachman four gold coins and says, "please follow me Capitán."

"Gracias, Señores," the coachman happily says as he begins to leave the palace.

The palace guard escorts them through the large palace and takes them to their chamber. Alejandro and Javier take in the view with awe as they scan the Royal paintings that hang on the walls of the spacious hallways.

The guard gets them to the chamber that is assigned to them and says, "Here you are, Viva El Rey Y Reina de España."

"Viva El Rey y Reina, guard," Capitán says as he properly salutes his contemporary.

Javier opens the door and they see several attendants standing in the very large room. The palace tailor takes measurements with his assistant while two maids draw hot baths for them to get prepared for tonight's special occasion. Once the tailor gets his measurements, he hands them over to the maids. The maids get them inside the baths and scrub them down with aromatic soaps and sweet-smelling oils to penetrate their tough skin. They experience the pampered treatment that the king and all his royal dignitaries receive daily in his royal court.

After they bathe, the maids get started on the intensive grooming with haircuts, manicures, and pedicures. Javier tries to resist the pedicure—there is nothing manly about this type of grooming.

"Be still," the maid firmly says, "you have to look your best if you are to stand before His Majesty's presence!"

"Relax, amigo." El Capitán says, "You've heard the saying, when in Rome..."

"Do as the Romans do," Javier says as he sulks in displeasure.

"Soon, we'll be back to our rugged-sailor lifestyle."

Once they finish the pedicures, they receive hot towels to their face to prepare for a shave on their faces and massages to help them unwind before the ball starts to take place.

After hours of receiving the pampering ordered by the king himself, the tailor shows up with the garments fitted for the ball. The palace tailor took the standard-issue naval uniforms and put his special touch on them to make them look royally presentable.

When they finished getting dressed, they hear a knock on the door and a lovely young lady enters the chamber. She gives them a bow and says, "My name is Princess Fatima, I am the King's niece. His Majesty has tasked me with the pleasure of escorting you to the ballroom. His Highness will send for you when he's ready to require your presence."

They both take a bow and El Capitán says, "Thank you Princess, it is a pleasure to be escorted by such beauty."

She extends her right hand and they both take a turn kissing her hand.

"Oh, Capitán." she says blushfully, "You are so charming."

"Only when blessed with such beauty," he replies.

They follow her as she gracefully maneuvers through the maze of the palace hallways that lead to the exquisite ballroom. These two humble men have never been a part of anything this extravagant.

"Wow!" Javier manages to mumble.

"Wow is the perfect description, amigo," El Capitán says.

"Caballeros," Fatima says, "Please enjoy His Majesty's graciousness towards all his subjects."

She walks away and heads towards her friends to chat with them. The nicely played music gets people to gracefully glide across the room as they dance the night away. Alejandro and Javier see a few acquaintances that are in attendance and they give a few nods to acknowledge them.

"Capitán De Los Amantes," a man standing behind him says.

Just hearing the voice of the man causes him to shrug in annoyance. He turns around to see his old Captain, Admiral Rodriguez. The short Admiral looks up to cut El Capitán down to his height with a look of pure disdain.

"Oh, Admiral," El Capitán says as he pretends to expect to see someone else eye-to eye when he turns.

"If it isn't my most finest sailor. I see you have finally arrived. Welcome to society's most elite."

"Yes, it's nice."

The Admiral signals him to come closer and says, "I will never forget Vera Cruz. I will keep a close eye on you, Capitán."

"Admiral, por favor, please excuse my zealous ignorance, I was muy joven y estupido."

"You disobeyed my orders and embarrassed me before my men!"

"I know and I beg you, disculpa me. You have to admit it, it did work out for the both of us, you got your own fleet and I got out of the little hair you have left."

"Go to el infierno, Capitán!" The Admiral mumbles as he storms away while taking tiny steps.

"Guillermo told you," Javier says.

"Por favor, not now Javier."

"His wrath for you will never be appeased until he sees you buried in the ground," Javier finishes saying.

"The best time of my youth was being able to disobey his cowardice commands."

"It was mucho gusto for me as well, let's just hope it does not come back to bite us on our buttocks."

"Please tell me Javier, why do the cowardice receive all the accolades that the brave accomplish?"'

"They don't receive it. They purchase it with gold and seal it with their bloodlines," Javier replies.

"That is a wise saying, Amigo, a very wise saying."

A waiter stops by and allows them to get a couple of glasses of Champagne imported from France's finest vineyards to make a toast to a loyal and trusting friendship. Two lovely maidens cross their paths and they take on their requests to test the dance floor. They twist and turn while they gently allow the music to guide their every step to the mellow sound. They politely bow down to their partners when the song finishes. Shortly after that, there becomes a stirring from the crowd as everyone begins to draw their attention towards the ballroom entrance.

"Señoras y Caballeros, I present you El Principe de España and his future bride to be," the announcer says with a grandiose voice.

The crowd immediately splits in half and clap their hands to welcome in the newly engaged couple as they walk into the grand ballroom. El Capitán's heart takes a quick rest from beating when he recognizes the woman the prince is engaged to. His eyes cannot believe that the only woman his heart has ever yearned for is standing before him.

She graciously receives the warm reception while El Capitán oddly stares at her. Her beauty is so captivating, her every step seems as if she's not even touching the ground. Her brunette hair has soft curls to compliment the cutest dimples one can see when she smiles. Her light brown eyes allow onlookers access to see her inner-soul and all its pureness.

Alejandro is in an unbelief trance and Javier is watching his dear friend awkwardly stare at the guest of honor. For a brief moment, the thought of daring to shut his Captain's jaw-dropped mouth crosses his mind.

"Are you ok, Capitán?" Javier asks.

"Catalina," is the only word that manages to escape his lips.

Catalina was the love of Alejandro's teenage life. Her father, a royal dignitary, and infatuated with maintaining that lifestyle refused to accept his daughter falling in love with the butcher's son. He arranged for Catalina to be sent away to The Royal Palace and had his servants hurt Alejandro the night the two were supposed to leave to the New World. That night left Alejandro with a broken heart to go with his cracked ribs and split lip. The only way to heal from this crushing ordeal was to take his destiny into his own hands and follow Guillermo into the Spanish Navy. The seas and all the wild adventures it contains helped subside his natural feelings for Catalina. Ten years later, Alejandro realizes that his love for her still remains very much alive. He takes a few seconds to snap out of it and decide whether or not he should greet her, but the master butler intrudes on that decision.

"The King and Queen request your presence, Capitán," the butler says with his head up high, it's as if he is keeping his nose from dripping.

"Who is she Capitán?" Javier asks as they follow the butler.

"She's just a childhood friend, amigo."

"Por Favor, don't do it, Capitán."

"Do what Javier?"

"You know what, she's not worth it! Mi Cabeza works best when it's still attached to my body!"

"If you insist, amigo."

"I very much insist, Capitán."

The butler gets them to the entrance that is guarded by two men. They make way and allow the three to enter the King's quarters.

"Your Highness, Capitán Alejandro De Los Amantes and Executive Officer Javier Lopez of your Royal Naval Force," the butler says as all three bow before the King and Queen.

"Welcome Capitán," the King says, "your brave and noble service is very much welcome. Your King is very gracious."

The King is a couple of inches shorter than El Capitán, but his build is intimidating with his broad shoulders and protruding chest. A large crown rests on his head with a slight tilt to the left.

The Queen walks over to her subjects and extends her hand to El Capitán and he reaches for it to gently plant his lips on it.

"You are of supreme beauty, mi Reyna."

She smiles while she blushes from his soothing compliment.

Her insecurity causes layers of makeup to be put on her face in order to help disguise her imperfections.

He reaches inside his garment and plucks a parchment roll out of it. He hands it to the King and says, "This map leads you to the lost Incan City of Gold that sits on The Sacred Lake."

"You have been proven to be a great asset to my kingdom. It is true what they say?"

"What might that be, my Lord?"

"You are better than twenty of the best Seadogs that Inglatierra has to offer."

"Your Highness has given his humble servant worthy seamen. These worthy seamen are the only reason I am able to stand before you to receive such praise."

"Do you hear your Capitán, XO Lopez? He hands over his praise to his subordinates."

"Si, my Lord, he's a man of loyalty and honor. The greatest man I ever met."

"The greatest?" The King asks.

"After you, my lord. I owe my life a thousand times to him. He has taught me countless times that the greatest honor one can have is serving a gracious and righteous King."

"Is that so?"

"Si, your Majesty," Javier replies.

The Queen takes a trip around El Capitán's body and touches the tip of his chin and says, "The rumors of your beauty are more than true."

"Gracia, mi Reyna, but your beauty is far better than any treasure the New World has to offer my King."

"Very well," the King says with a tiny jealous tone, "My Queen, please excuse us while I attend to the business at hand."

The Queen walks away with a stare that is directed towards Alejandro with the corner of her eye. "Don't take too long, mi amor, our son awaits us."

"Buenos noche, mi Reyna," Alejandro and Javier each say as they bow again.

"I have a mission for you Capitán," the King says as his Queen leaves the room, "I want this to be between us and no one else."

"We are gracious to serve you, your Majesty."

"The Governor of Mexico has made a great discovery. They found the map of the Secret Temple that is said to contain the Armor of Monteczuma."

"Por favor, my Lord, that treasure is a myth, it does not exist."

"So you do not believe the Story of the Aztecs making one last stand to wisk away that treasure without leaving a clue to the trail?"

"No, I am sorry, but I do not. It was all fabricated to get your Majesty to chase fictitious dreams," El Capitán replies.

"How about you, XO Lopez, do you believe in it?"

"I've never heard such a tale," Javier replies.

"Well, this treasure exists." the King says as he hands him the map, "And I want you to sail to the Yucatán Peninsula and lead the expedition."

While the King speaks, El Capitán's attention begins to focus on Catalina. He silently asks himself what does she see in the weak and spoiled prince. He's not worthy of Catalina's love and touch.

"Capitán, are you listening?" the King asks.

"Claro, my Lord, I'll accept your duty on a few conditions."

"State your request, servant."

"If this leyenda is true, this is a treasure like no other, and the greatest to ever be discovered. I want Villas for I and my men. We want to be able to retire in peace and in God's humble grace. I also want you to uphold this promise for the family of those who may lose their lives on this dangerous quest, my Lord."

"Once again, you share your glory with your subordinates; I can respect a loyal trait."

"My loyalty is just an extension of my Lord's grace towards all his subjects."

"Your request is granted, but should you fail, all will suffer death."

"I will not have it any other way, my Lord. I and my men will leave tomorrow to accomplish your task, my Lord."

"Whatever you need, take with you, it is at your disposal."

"Thank you, my Lord."

"Very well, you may be dismissed," the King says as he signals them to leave.

"Viva el Rey del España."

They both bow and leave the King's quarters to head back to the ball.

"What is this Armor of Monteczuma?" Javier asks.

"It is an armor believed to have special powers that command the indestructible Army of the Underworld. Guillermo told me this tale when I first joined the Navy."

"So this armor really doesn't exist?"

The Aztecs were afraid of the Spaniards getting their hands on it. And the leyenda has it, that they were able to sneak it out of the capital when the Conquistadors kidnapped Monteczuma. They hid it in a secret temple they call Death. It is guarded by evil spirits so that no one can come near the golden armor. Whoever possesses the armor can be ruler or destroyer of the world."

"And you decided to sail one last time to retrieve such a treasure?"

"Si, you leave tonight to gather the men. Prepare the ship for our final voyage. Then we are free men, we can finally grow old and get fat like we always dreamed Javier."

Javier shakes his head as he eases Alejandro's hands off his shoulders and says," I hate that grin of yours."

"What grin?" Alejandro asks as he continues to give him a rakish smile.

"Alejandro?" Catalina says as she runs into them. "Is that you Alejandro Maldonado?"

"Maldonado?" Javier asks.

"Yes, hello my dear Catalina. I guess congratulations are in order. el principe cannot do any better than you."

"Hola. And who might this be?" she asks as she looks at Javier.

"This is my first mate, Executive officer Javier Lopez. A great sailor and a far better amicable companion."

"Hola Señorita. Did you call him Maldonado?"

"Yes, I did. That is his given surname," she replies.

"Is that so?" he says as he tries to step in front of El Capitán.

"Please forgive my amigo, the champagne has his head heavy. Don't you have somewhere to go Javier?"

"Oh yes, duties call me. Señorita," he says as he eases past Catalina.

"Hasta mañana, Javier. Please safeguard this map as well."

Javier grabs the map and takes two steps behind Catalina. He makes a gesture of one's head being cut off to remind him to keep his word. Catalina feels a swift movement behind her and she turns around to see what the commotion is all about. Javier quickly straightens up, smiles, and walks away.

El Capitán just stands there with a nervous smile while his palms get sweaty and his stomach flutters like butterflies in the midst of spring.

"And your friend?" she asks as she turns back towards Alejandro.

"For a sailor, he's not a good swimmer, and too much time underneath the water damaged his cabeza—I should have let him drown.

She shakes her head at his response.

"You truly deserve to be the bride of the King's heir."

"Oh, Alejandro, please stop." she says as she nudges him.

"I mean it, you still look amazing."

"I see your way with words never change."

"Well," he says as he shrugs.

"But you've changed a lot. You changed your name and looks. I barely recognized you."

"So how did you?" he asks as the nerves in his gut ease up.

"Your ojos. They make any room come to life. You know, I spoke to your Madre recently."

"You have, what did she say?"

The Prince finally finds his fiancé and decides to intrude on their conversation. Suddenly, the feeling of being possessive overwhelms the Prince as he surveils the friendly interaction between the two.

"My dear, I have been looking all over for you," he says as he puts an uncomfortable hand on her back, "Hola Capitán, I see you are enjoying the occasion."

"Si, I'm just catching up with an old friend."

"So you two know each other," the Prince asks.

"Yes Miguel," Catalina says, "Alejandro's Father served my household with the finest cuts of beef and pork."

"Oh, a butcher, that's such a brutish trade."

The comment made by the snobbish prince causes El Capitán to grind his teeth. Instead of indulging into the remark, he decides to say, "Please forgive me your Highness, I do not want to hold you any longer, the affairs of your father await me. Catalina."

"Alejandro, take care and say hello to your mother for me."

"I will do so."

El Capitán walks away as fast as he can while a sharp pain shoots in his chest. His heart starts to long for her love. Maybe, he thinks to himself, one touch will be enough to suffice his unobtainable desire.

The prince walks back towards the ballroom with a grin on his face. He does not like what his eyes just witnessed. He was once told, by his gossiping twin cousins, that Catalina's heart could never be owned because it belonged to a butcher's son. His persistence to have everything, shunned that oblivious notion while he continued his pursuit to obtain her. At first, Catalina did not show the Prince any interest, but she eventually gave in. She had come to the realization that love does not have a place in Spain's high society.

Now the Prince has a real dilemma on his hands. He knows his father has great ambitions and El Capitán is the only man to carry them out. He also knows that his relationship with Catalina is still in its infancy stage and El Capitán's quick rise up in the naval ranks is infringing on that relationship.

He acts swiftly and motions for Fatima to come to his aid.

"What," she mouths out from across the room.

"Come quickly," he replies in the same manner.

She walks over to him and finds out what the emergency is.

"I need your help, Cousin."

"Whatever you ask, my Lord."

"It's time to play our lovely game."

"Who are we going to oust, my Lord," she asks in joy.

"We are going to oust El Capitán," he replies.

"But my Lord, he has special orders from our King."

"I need you to do it!" he says in a demanding voice and then cracks a fake grin when people pass them by.

"I want you to have the bartender spike his drink and have the number to his chamber switched with yours. When he stumbles into your room, I want you to accuse him of attempting to defile your innocence."

She does as told and gives the bartender the signal to indicate her target. Fatima and Miguel are known for executing scandalous plots to get anyone they dislike to get removed from the King's Court. It's all a game to them and the thrill makes them callous to the seriousness of the lives they play with.

El Capitán sits down and he sulks at the bar internally. He asks for a shot of rum to help numb the heartache. After his second shot, he feels a bit woozy and his eyes produce double vision. He gets off the stool and decides to call it a night; it's been awhile since he had rum this good. He makes his way back to his assigned quarter with a drunken stumble all the way there. He opens the door and hops on the bed.

"Ahhhh," exclaims Fatima, "Help!" She jumps up and runs out of her room with her gown torn while El Capitán's face shows an expression of confusion before he passes out. The guards get her attention as she points inside her room.

"He's in there! He tried to defile me!"

They run into the room while a crowd develops outside the hallway to see what the fuss is all about. They pull out El Capitán while he tries to fight the effects of the drug that was put in his drink. The entire crowd gasps for air when they see who it is.

The two guards drag him down to the dungeon and shackle him to the wall next to another prisoner that awaits his fate in the King's Court. The news of El Capitán's arrest spreads like fire across the land of España. It reached the men just before Javier arrived to give them their new orders. The men act fast and head back to retrieve their Captain. They know with all their heart that those charges are false and El Capitán is in dire need of saving.

El Capitán wakes up the next day and finds himself feeling groggy and chained to a wall. He struggles to free himself. His state of confusion is at an all time high as he tries to make sense of his situation. He tries to free himself again, but to no avail.

"They will not give way, trust me, I've tried." the prisoner next to him says.

"It's you."

"Yes, it's me, your prisoner."

The captured pirate is badly hurt with cuts and bruises all over his face and body as he barely hangs on the wall.

"Guard! Guard!"

The guard comes to his attention and says, "Silencio!"

"But there must be some…" he says.

"Smack!" rings out as the guard backhands El Capitán.

"I said silencio!"

The guard walks out of the cell while El Capitán waits for the feeling to come back to the right side of his face.

"The buzz around here is that their famous Capitán attempted to defile the King's niece."

"That is false!"

"Whether it is false or not, those are your charges, Signoré. Welcome to the wrong side of an oppressive State."

Catalina walks in with an upset look on her face. Her puffed up face indicates that she also spent some time crying.

"Oh Catalina, Gracia a Dios you're here!"

She steps in and slaps him in the face as she yells. "How could you?!"

"Por favor, Catalina, you have to believe me, 1 would never do such a thing!"

"Silencio Alejandro! Fatima told me everything! You are willing to make my Lord's niece a liar to keep your reputation intact?! To think, I once loved you!"

She turns her back and runs away with tears escaping her eyelids. She feels a sensation of betrayal as she runs to find Miguel to be consoled by him. She gets to his chamber door and she hears chuckles escape the cracked door.

"Oh Cousin! You should've seen poor Catalina's face when I broke the bad news to her! She was so distraught!" Fatima says after she mimicked Catalina's genuine concern.

"Gracias, Fatima. Now all I have to do is console her and she will finally belong to me!"

Catalina's mind races three different ways; she's shocked, confused, and disgusted at the same time. Alejandro was telling the truth all along. It was just one of the Prince's evil plots to obtain her love. She tries to find the King to put a stop to this, but the Prince hears footsteps and notices Catalina eavesdropping on his conversation. He catches Catalina a few yards away as she slips and stumbles in the hallway.

"I will not marry you!" she exclaims as he tries to help her up.

"You will marry me, because if you don't, your family will suffer the consequence!"

"I will not suffice to your manipulative vices!"

"That's too bad, you would have made a great Reina! He will die, your family will lose favor in this court and you will be cast out in shame! Guards, take this traitor and lock her in the palace's North Tower. Keep her from my Father's presence until his Court is adjourned!"

"Alejandro will thwart your childish plot. He is a better man than you'll ever be!" she yells out loud as she gets hauled away.

***

El Capitán patiently hangs quietly as he awaits the demise of his sham trial.

"So," the prisoner says, "that was an awkward situación. My name is Ronaldo Insidioso of Sicilia."

"Hola, Ronaldo."

"So please tell me, who was that beautiful woman who blessed you with that slap to the face?"

"Catalina," he replies.

"Well I know that much, tell me mas."

"We were once in love when we were young back in our hometown, Seville."

"You know, you seem real at ease. In fact, for a man who's about to die, too much at ease."

"The King will come to his senses and vindicate me."

"Ha! Ha! Ha!"

"What is so funny?" El Capitán asks as he angrily stares at him.

"You think the King will side with you over his Sangre? You are delusional, Signoré!"

"Well, if that's the case, then my men will save me."

"Your men are that loyal?"

"I should hope so. I would do so for them. We are nothing like you lawless pirates."

"How about me? May I come with you?"

"Oh, Amigo, I wish you could, but I have no dealings with thieving pirates and enemigos of España."

"That's ironic! Ha! Ha!"

"What do you laugh at?"

"Look around you, you might be a loyal and righteous sailor, but España has you pegged as an enemigo as well. Yet you hang here and judge me for my mistake. In the eyes of your blessed King, you are scum to him as well as I am."

"You are right, Amigo," El Capitán says.

He takes a few seconds to think his situation through. All the hard work that he has strived to achieve—honor, integrity and respect—is now going down the royal drain.

"No matter what happens, my service to España has expired. You can come along as well if you swear to valiantly stand by me and my men with honor at all times."

"You have my word, Capitán."

A maid rushes into the cell and interrupts the brief male-bonding. She's breathing very heavily as she tries to regain enough wind to speak.

"Capitán," she exclaims, "I am Señorita Catalina's maid. The prince has her locked away in the palace's North Tower. She knows the truth about your charges!"

Two guards walk in and nudge the maid to the side to get to the prisoners.

"Are you two ready to answer to Dios for your sins?" one jokingly asks.

"Dios will have nothing to do with them," the other says. "They are going straight to El infierno!"

"No, no," says the maid. "This is a terrible mistake, he's innocente!"

"Step away Señorita or we will charge you with obstruction of justice!!" the first guard says.

She moves out of the way as she hopelessly watches the two prisoners get dragged away.

"I will come for her!" El Capitán exclaims as he makes his way towards the King.

He mouths out a prayer that his mother taught him when he was young. Ronaldo tries to squirm, kick and resist the strong guard's grip as much as he can, but it is to no avail. He must answer to the King for his crime as well.

The guards finally get to the center of the King's royal court and they force the prisoners on the ground. El Capitán and Ronaldo stay prostate to help gain some kind of mercy from the King and Queen. The spectators mumble as they watch the noble sailor's reputation hit rock bottom.

"Your Majesty, Ruler of España and her precious territories, chosen by Dios to be Ruler of the land, we stand before you with two complaints," the Royal Scribe reads out loud from the scroll.

"Please state the charges of these offenders, Scribe," the king arrogantly says.

"We have a thief," the Scribe says as he points to Ronaldo, "Who conspired with a known enemy of the state, El Tiburón, to steal your Majesty's royal treasure. His name is Ronaldo Insidioso of Sicilia. He was arrested by this man, Capitán Alejandro De Los Amantes."

"Ahhh," sighs the King, "the irony of this situation. The thief is sentenced to death. Now, tell me Scribe, what is El Capitán's charge."

"He is accused of attempting to defile Princess Fatima, Your Highness," the Scribe replies.

The crowd begins to stir and the whispers fill the air. The King gets upset from the noise being made and disappointed in El Capitán's charge. He takes a deep breath and then makes a gesture to settle down the crazed audience.

"Silencio!" the King demands as his subjects take heed to it. "My dear niece, is this true?"

"Si, my lord, it is all true," she replies in a dramatic tone.

"Capitán De Los Amantes, you are a citizen of España, a man who is deemed to be of code and honor, what say you of these charges?"

"Your majesty, I am innocent of these trumped up charges. Had I any urge to pursue your Niece, Your Highness, a simple request by you would have sufficed, am I not correct?"

"You are most certain, Capitán," the King replies.

"Your highness, this is a plot to dispose of your most humble servant. The heir of your throne is behind this atrocious plot and for what reasons…"

"Enough!" the Prince exclaims as he steps forward and strikes El Capitán with the palm of his hand. "How can you slander my name and embarrass this Kingdom with your doggish manners!"

"If my ways are so doggish, why do you keep a witness that can exonerate me locked away!?"

The Prince tries to rush El Capitán to attack him, but the guards stand in the Prince's way.

"Stop!" the King yells, "who is this witness?"

"It is…" El Capitán tries to say.

In the midst of all the commotion a woman steps forward to get the King's attention.

"What business do you have, Magdalena?"

"My Lord, I watched the whole incident take place. El Capitán is guilty of the charge; anything else is just lies by this perro del mar!"

The crowd goes into an uproar while shock runs through all their veins—their famous Capitán looks guilty.

"Order in my Court," he exclaims as he pounds his staff, "I will have order in my Court!"

The King's hand is forced; he does not want to dig any further to uncover the truth. His Mistress, Magdalena, has drawn the line in the sand and he makes his decision after she speaks.

"Capitán De Los Amantes, I find you guilty of the charges and I sentence you to death by hanging. Where is the map to the Secret Temple?"

"Executive Officer Lopez obtains it, my Lord," El Capitán replies as he begins to see how corrupt the King's Court truly is.

"He will carry out my orders and assume your duties as Capitán of your ship. It deeply saddens me to mete out this punishment, but the severe nature of your crime leaves me no choice. Guards, take these men and have them executed."

El Capitán and Ronaldo try their best to resist their despised trip to the hangman's gallows. The only thing on Alejandro's mind is the fate of Catalina as he gets dragged away.

"At least the King heard you out, Signoré," Ronaldo says as his legs give way and no longer resist.

The four guards exit the Royal Court with the prisoners and they end up being surrounded by El Capitán's valiant men. Their swords are drawn and the palace guards do not put up a fight.

"What took you so long, Javier?"

"I was really contemplating the promoción," he replies with a smile as he unshackles him.

"I was beginning to think you were never going to show up."

"I see you've worn out your welcome with His Majesty."

"Free him as well, he comes with us!"

"This criminal?!" Octavio asks.

"In case you haven't noticed, we are criminals as well. We don't have much time and we don't leave anyone behind!"

Rogelio tosses a sword to El Capitán and he swoops it from mid-air and he leads his men to find Catalina.

"Where are we going? The exit is this way," Edwin says as he points left.

"To find Catalina!" he proudly says.

"Catalina?! Who is Catalina?!" Crissino asks.

"The Señorita," Javier replies.

"It's always a Señorita, will it ever stop?" Crissino says as he shakes his head while following his Capitán.

El Capitán and his rebel band fearlessly take on the King's guards as they march forward to get to the North Tower. The distress bell sounds off and troops gather as El Capitán explores unchartered territory; committing treason and aiding criminals.

They get to the North Tower and easily overtake the two guards. Javier sees his chance to strike a deadly blow.

"No," El Capitán says as he stops him, "We are not murderers, let them live!"

He opens the entrance, takes one of the overmatched guard's sword away, and walks up the stairs to find Catalina. He finds her pacing the tower in anxiousness. She turns herself around and wraps her arms around him when she realizes it is him.

"You're alive!"

He pulls her closely and presses his lips up against hers and lands the most passionate kiss. Perhaps, it is the final kiss they each get before they plunge to their death while they try to claw their way out of the palace.

"I hope your fencing skills are up-to-date, mi amor," he says as he hands her a sword.

"They are still far superior than your skills!" she replies.

"We must hurry, time is against us!"

They fight their way side-by-side and they reach the outer court of the palace. They get met by the King and his heralded infantry standing behind him. Their rifles are pointed directly at them and they are ready to fire.

"Traitors! You are all traitors! How dare you defy your righteous King?!"

"I am sorry, Your Highness, your laws are too burdensome! There is a double-standard between your subjects and your own flesh and blood!"

"Kill them all!" The King exclaims in an unbearable angry tone.

The infantry takes aim, and just before the infantry takes fire, Tuyen and Pho toss home-made explosives and cause the infantry to scatter. The King runs in terror and it allows El Capitán, Catalina, and his men to escape death as the Chinamen Twins continually toss explosions to confuse the infantry. They make their way to the King's stable and release all the horses they don't need and Guillermo sets the stable on fire.

They hop on the horses and ride west to get back to their ship and leave España once and for all.

As they sail west on the Atlantic Ocean, Javier asks, "What is next, Capitán?"

"We still have the map, right?"

"I have it here," he replies as he pats his chest.

He is holding on to Catalina with the intention of never letting go. They watch the sun melt away over the Western horizon and he says, "Then we sail to Mexico, Amigo!'

The Armor of Monteczuma

Deeply embedded in The Yucatán jungle is a treasure like no other and the power within Monteczuma'a Armor is too dangerous for anyone to grasp. The fate of the world rests in the hands of one man and his rebel band. Here lies the tale of the greatest treasure ever found; jewels upon jewels and a vast amount of gold abound...

The King is at the Royal palace having a royal tantrum on full display. The way things have just recently transpired with the failed execution and escape of El Capitán has him very angry and embarrassed. He hurls very large tomes across the room at his most trusted advisors and the head of the Royal guard.

"How could you allow this to happen, Ruperto?! In my own Palace! Your men are vile and incompetent! I want his head! I want it on a platter for all to see what the reward for treachery is in my Kingdom! I am not to be defied! Now, where is my spoiled Son?!"

"My men are accomplishing that command, my Lord." Ruperto replies in a frightened tone, "Soon, they will be here with him."

Along with the Head of the Royal guard are four other men that sit as advisors to the Administrative Affairs of Spain. The first is Foreign Minister, Sergio De Los Santos, the second is Minister of defense, Epifaño Maria Sanchez. Then there's Chief Naval officer Admiral Jamie Luis Rodriguez and the most trusted advisor to the King, Adolfo Cervantes of Madrid.

They each sit in their chairs patiently and quietly while they watch their Monarch pace back and forth in the Chamber. The door slowly cracks open and Principe Miguel tries to slowly ease his way into the Chamber. The King hears the hinges of the door pierce his ears and he charges his son like a crazed bull. He wraps his large hands around the prince's delicate neck while he slams him against the door violently. The prince starts to fight for air as he tries to process the warranted onrush.

"Embece!" The King furiously says, "Why was your future bride locked away in the Palace Tower?!"

The fierce grip on his Son does not allow him to speak. The prince's face is about to explode, so the King eases his grip for a brief moment to get him to spill out the words he desperately wants to hear.

"I... I... I found her giving information to an English spy. The spy escaped and I did not want to trouble you until all the facts were gathered."

"Lies!" The King says as he resumes choking his Son while drawing closer to him. "These are all lies! Admit it! Your childish insecurities caused a spat of jealousy to abound! Now I have to clean up your mess once again you spoiled brat! You have caused an embarrassment to this Kingdom, and thus, jeopardized its great existence!"

Adolfo steps in to help ease the situation between the two and says, "Por favor, My Lord, you are going too far!"

The King's rage has overtaken him very rapidly, but the voice of Adolfo seems to penetrate the red-seeing anger for a brief moment.

"Leave!" he says, "Leave before I take away your putrid life!"

Prince Miguel storms away with the feeling of disgrace running through his veins. His father has never corrected him in front of anyone in a public setting such as this and his emotions draw him back and forth as he vividly replays the last five minutes in his mind. Halfway through the journey back towards his quarters, he draws his sword and dares to let the thought of taking his father's life cross his mind.

He angrily steps back and forth in rage as he allows the thoughts to flow freely in his head. He takes a couple of deep breaths and comes to his senses and resumes his initial journey while he stores that thought in the back of his mind for another time.

Back in the Chambers, the King straightens himself up and takes twenty deep breaths to calm down and re-evaluate the entire situation at hand.

"Ruperto," he says.

"Si, My Lord," he replies.

"Place two guards in front of my Son's quarters. He is not to leave until I deem it necessary."

"As you command, My Lord." he says while he bows before he leaves.

"Well," the King says as he addresses the rest, "What do you propose we do about this dilemma that we are in?"

"El Capitán is a very skilled sailor, My Lord," Epifañio says. "His act of tración can spread very fast and it can be a threat to the safeguard of your Kingdom. We must act swiftly and put an end to it before this treacherous fire devours your legacy, Your Highness."

"How do you suppose we do so?" The King asks.

"May I speak, your Highness?" Admiral Rodriguez asks.

"You have permission, Admiral."

"Alejandro De Los Amantes spent seven years under my command. Everything he has learned as a sailor was spent under my tutelage. He's the finest sailor I've seen, but he is reckless and I know his careless tactics. Please allow me to sail and put an end to El Capitán's rebellion before it becomes too late."

"He learned everything from you except cowardice," Epifañio mumbles under his breath.

"What was that Commander Sanchez?" the king asks.

"Nada, My Lord." he replies, "just a sore throat."

The Admiral understood the mumble and his stare cut his Superior Officer in half. The feud between these two dates back to their adolescent years when they first swore to fight for the Kingdom's cause.

"As I was saying, Your Majesty, I will retrieve El Capitán and lead the expedition to the Temple of Muerte personally."

"We must also be careful not to make him a martyr to those who wish to resist your gracious policies, my Lord," Sergio De Los Santos says.

"You are right," the King said, "We must erase his entire existence and exclude him from any of our military Campaigns, including Vera Cruz."

After he speaks, he thinks about his son's irrational act and how it has caused havoc in his Court. Time after time, he has stood idle on his son's theatrics; hoping his immaturity will eventually subside. Now his inaction forces him to display a show of immovable strength towards his most beloved subject to keep his legacy intact.

"Epifañio, you will sail with Admiral Rodriguez and lead the expedition to the Temple of Muerte. The Governor of Mexico has a second copy of the map secured at his estate. Make sure you do everything possible to eradicate El Capitán and his ship."

"As you command, My Lord." Epifañio says.

"Now go! Time is against us! Find me that treasure and find me El Capitán!"

Epifaño and Admiral Rodriguez give each other disdain looks, but they walk in unison as they put their mutual hatred to the side for the time being. The Kingdom is in a state of distress and their petty bickering has to be put on a shelf right now.

"Minister De Los Santos, you are to engage in peace talks with England. We will have to stall our initial campaign against that vile Queen."

"Claro, My Lord." he replies and then he steps out of the room.

The only two standing in the Chamber is the King and his brother-in-law, Adolfo. The look on Adolfo's face is all too familiar.

"Not now, Adolfo."

"My dear friend, how long have we known each other?"

"Not long enough," the King replies, "But if you must be entertained by your King, then I'll say it—"

"Your Majesty," he says as he stops the King short, "I only live to serve you, and your grace is more than your servant deserves. I came from the slums of Madrid, and you have blessed me with the privilege of my seeds being called prince and princess in your Royal Court, My Lord. I can die tonight a happy man."

"What am I to do with my Son? He has grown to be spoiled and impetuous. I have failed, O Adolfo, I have failed as a father."

"Stop feeling sorry for yourself, mi Rey. He is his father's Son. You were exactly the same way when we first met. It was not until that successful battle in Lisbon that forged you to become a great King today."

"So, what are you saying?"

"Give him a campaign to help him grow up and seize his rightful claim to be your heir," Adolfo replies.

The King sighs as he takes in Adolfo's counsel very deeply. He recalls his youth and thinks hack to how firm his father viciously handled him and now he finally understands why.

"He's too soft, Adolfo."

"That only makes him easier to mold under fire. He must learn to understand the importance of every Subject's life, they are not his to be toyed with and discarded for his pleasure."

"You have razón, mi hermano, and you have convinced me to take heed to your consejo. Please go and prepare your nephew for his campaign."

***

Back on "El Amante Del Mar", they are three days into their voyage as they sail towards Spain's territories in the New World. El Capitán gathers his men's attention and says, "Please hear me, my fellow Sailors. I owe everyone on this ship my life and you have my upmost gratitude for that wonderful display of courage. Due to your undying loyalty, we are no longer welcomed by our homeland. We have been branded as vandals and rebels to España."

"So are we pirates?" Edwin asks.

"No," El Capitán replies, "We shall never become such a vile group of sailors. We will sail for a greater cause."

"And what cause shall that be, Capitán?" Guillermo asks.

"I'm not quite sure," El Capitán says as he rubs his chin, "But it will represent truth and righteousness and our souls will be bound by it!"

"And our mission?" Javier asks.

"I have a map that leads us to the Temple of Muerte. If any of you do not wish to go forth on this mission, you can leave this ship when we hit land."

"What is this Temple of Death?" Crissino asks.

"This secret temple," El Capitán replies, " is said to have the Armor of Monteczuma and its most prized treasure of the Aztecs."

"That treasure does not exist!" Pablo exclaims as he tries to secure his eye patch and fix his oversized bridges. "It's just a fictitious folklore to instigate the thirst of greedy pirates!"

"That treasure does exist, Pablo!" Guillermo exclaims with a sure tone in his voice.

"How can such a seasoned sailor be so gullible?!"

Pablo and Guillermo each take a step towards each other as Guillermo says, "What did you spill out of your foolish mouth?!"

"That's enough!" Javier says as he steps between the two of them.

"Capitán," Guillermo says, "we must not disturb the evil that dwells in that temple."

"I am well aware of that leyenda, my old friend, but the King cannot have this treasure. His character is compromised by his favor towards his heir and his ultimate greed. If this leyenda is true, that armor must be safely guarded from men such as the King."

"They will come for us," Rogelio says.

"And they will hit us with everything they got to exterminate us," Javier says as he finishes the pilot's thoughts.

"We have two things on our side; one, that has never stopped us before; and two, we know who is coming for us."

"I'm in," Edwin says.

"Who else is with me?" El Capitán asks.

The crew takes a brief moment to glance at each other and get the other's approval. "We will!" the crew yells out loud in unison as they stomp their feet in happiness.

"To glory! " Rogelio the Moor exclaims, "And to el Mar!"

"Viva la Mar!" They all chant, "Viva la Mar!"

Catalina sneaks out of El Capitán's quarters to find out what is happening on the ship's deck, Alejandro turns around and sees her uncomfortably watching the sailors celebrate. He walks towards her to have the talk he's been putting off since the day they left Spain for good.

They go back inside his cabin and she says, "Your men truly adore you and they are very loyal."

"Yes," he replies, "Their valor is impeccable. España will mourn for their return one day. Mi mor, We must talk."

"Speak your mente, Alejandro."

"What do you expect from me, Catalina?"

"I expect for you to never leave my side," she replies.

"I have dreamed this in my sleep countless times, but I'm a sailor that's being hunted by my own King. Living life in these troubled seas is no place for a Señorita such as you. This wretched ship is my home and the list of its enemigos is burdensome."

"You should know me by now, Alejandro, I will not leave you! If this ship is your home, then it will sink with us together!"

"Mi Corazón belongs to you my dear."

"That's all that matters to me, mi amor," she says as she brushes her hand across his face, "And that's all we need to keep this vessel afloat. our love for each other will suffice."

Alejandro grabs hold of Catalina and he slowly kisses her. She breathes heavily as he picks her up and gently lays her on the bed.

"Will you marry me, Catalina," he whispers between kisses.

"Yes. Alejandro! I will marry you!"

***

Alejandro wakes up early the following morning and gathers himself up before he slowly steps out of the cabin without waking

Catalina up. He feels reinvigorated while he checks on the ship as he normally does so every early morning.

Ronaldo is piloting the ship and the rest of the deck is clear. El Capitán greets him with a swift motion of tipping his hat.

"Capitán," he says to acknowledge his Captain as he stays on course steering the ship.

"Don Insidioso, how is your stay so far on our humble abode?"

"Well," Ronaldo says at first and then shakes his head to not share his thought.

"Come on, Ronaldo," El Capitán says, "El Amante Del Mar is a ship that cherishes honesty over niceness."

"To be honest, Signoré, I still hear snickers when my back is turned and they leave when I enter, Capitán."

"You have to forgive them, they are still Spaniards at heart and Spaniards are very proud and stubborn."

"I just hope they find it in their hearts to forgive me."

"They will," El Capitán replies as he gives him a reassuring pat on his back, "They will do so when you prove yourself to be worthy of being trusted with their lives in your hands."

Javier comes on deck and he salutes his Superior Officer when he approaches them.

"At ease, Javier."

"Buenos dias, Capitán."

"Muy bien, it's time to run drills, so let's wake those lazy men up."

"As you command, Capitán."

He turns about as he ignores the presence of Ronaldo to go and awake the ship's crew.

"Javier."

"Si Capitán?" he asks.

"Never mind, I'll do it. Please relieve Ronaldo of his duty. Meet me down at the barracks when Rogelio comes on deck." He gives Javier a look that he knows all too well. That look is always given when a talk needs to be had eventually.

"Come with me, Ronaldo," El Capitán says as he heads down towards the Crew's barracks.

"So please tell me, Capitán, what is so dangerous about this Aztec treasure and why is it important to the King?"

Guillermo is coming up the ladder from the bottom deck and meets them on the middle deck. His grizzled face shows that there's not much left that life can throw at him.

"Guillermo," says El Capitán.

"Hola, Capitán. Hola Ronaldo," he instinctly says.

"Guillermo introduced me to the sea life and he's indispensible on this ship."

"Gracias, Capitán."

"If he introduced you, why is he not Captain?"

"I prefer to dwell behind the curtains of fame," he replies.

"Are the men still asleep?"

"All but your naive primo, Capitán."

"Ronaldo knows nothing of the leyenda of Monteczuma. Please kindly entertain us with this wonderful tale, Guillermo."

"Oh no. I kindly defer, Capitán."

"Please, you tell it the best. Guillermo is playing shy, Ronaldo, but he has a knack for storytelling."

"If you insist, Capitán. This treasure of the Aztecs is the most coveted in the entire world, old and new. Only the Garden of Eden will be a greater discovery for all of mankind.

"When Cortez marched his troops into the Capital of Tenochtitan and kidnapped Monteczuma. The priests secured the treasure and sent it away to be hidden in a secret temple. Along with all the fine jewels and gold was an Armor of special metal that is overlaid with solid gold. This armor is believed to harness the power of the Cosmos and summon an indestructible army from the underworld. The Aztecs used this Armor to conquer their neighboring foes to forge their empire in Mexico."

"If they had this Armor, how did Cortez siege the capital?" Ronaldo asks.

"The answer is twofold, amigo. When Monteczuma began to reign, he refused to wear the armor, he understood that its origin was intended for evil and because they also believed that Cortez's arrival was the fulfillment of the prophecy of their white god returning."

"Why must we be the ones to retrieve it?"

He gives El Capitán a look to gauge whether he's said too much and El Capitán says, "Keep going Guillermo."

"Whoever possesses the armor will be able to subdue the entire world into supreme submission. No man on earth will be able to righteously wear this armor because the heart of man is not pure. They will always choose destruction and vast amounts of innocent souls will be lost." He makes the sign of the Cross and then kisses his hand in great fear as he discloses the rest of the leyenda. "If we find this temple, we will have to answer to Las Lloronas."

"Las Lloronas?" Ronaldo says with a look of confusion.

"Si, they were once actual Souls, Madres to be exacto. During an Aztec ceremony, the ancient priest's accidently summoned demonios and they possessed the Mothers' souls and they began to drown their children in the capital's lake. People say that you can hear their demonic cries in the night near the Secret Temple. They call them Las Lloronas because they cry dark tears when they attack."

"And you believe this, Capitán?"

"Yes, I do," Alejandro replies. "The leyenda has been around for almost two centuries and is the most famoso in the New World. At first, I did not care if my King retrieved it, but his act of injustice towards me proves that he is unworthy of obtaining it."

"It sounds to me like Las Lloronas have it secured, so why must we go?" Ronaldo asks.

"We must be sure that no one claims this armor" El Capitán replies.

"Everything about this leyenda is true," Guillermo says, "I'm begging you Capitán, we must stay away from that temple or lives will be lost."

"The fate of el mundo depends on us. We cannot allow vain kings to attain such a power as that armor."

"As you…"

The bottom deck releases a commotion while Guillermo is saying his last words. The three men rush down the ladder to find out what exactly is going on. A few of the sailors are laughing as Crissino and Eduardo roll across the wooden floor in a tussle.

"Stop it," Octavio exclaims it as he tries to get involved.

"Let them be," Edwin says as he nudges Octavio towards the side.

El Capitán splits the crowd shoulders first and he breaks up the fight. He holds Eduardo while Guillermo stands up Crissino.

"What is going on?!" he asks between breaths.

"And why are your bridges soaked? " Guillermo asks behind El Capitán's question.

The rest of the crew laughs as Crissino makes another attempt to fight Eduardo.

"This idiot laid my hand in a bucket of warm water while I was asleep and it caused me to urinate on myself!"

Guillermo and El Capitán burst out in laughter while El Capitán lands a light-hearted fist on his left shoulder. Guillermo pats him on the other to get him to ease up on the prank by Eduardo.

"You are now an official member of this ship, Crissino. We should have done it sooner, but all the chaos caused us to forget."

"I tried to tell him, Capitán," Eduardo says. "But he just hit me."

"Alright men, settle down, that's how we ease tensions on this ship's daily grind Crissino. But you also know that there is no fighting, so the two of you will be on mop and laundry duty for two weeks."

"That's not fair, Capitán!" Eduardo says.

"You know the reglas, Eduardo; you fight, you suffer the consequences of those actions. Now get to your duties."

He watches the two leave the bottom deck and says, "Are there any more problems we need to address?"

The men stay silent.

"Good, Rogelio get to your post."

"As you command," Rogelio replies.

"Edwin, get started on today's meals. The rest of you are going to run cannon drills."

"Ahhh!" The men all say as if they are getting punished as well.

"Por favor, Capitán," Tuyen asks. "Why must we run drills?"

"We have another foe to add to our list of enemies and it's our King. I'm pretty sure that Veracruz is the most likely scenario we are going to face once again. Although, el Mano de Dios was on our side to lead us through, we must keep our sailing skills sharp."

"Veracruz?" Ronaldo says.

"It's a long story," Guillermo whispers to him. "It's part of the razón why we are in this situation."

"Let's get going," El Capitán says, "glory awaits us."

"To glory!" Pablo says.

"To glory!" They all yell. "Viva la Mar! "

The Chinamen Twins and Otavio are the first to get to the middle deck where the cannons are placed. They unload a barrel of gunpowder and prepare the fuse boxes while the others check the cannons. Javier makes his way down and quickly gets to his Captain to give him some news.

"Why is there a look of worry on your face?" El Capitán asks.

"Catalina is up and she refuses to stay in your quarters, Sir. She's adamant on being useful on this ship. I charged her with the duty of high watch."

"Orchestrate the drills. I'll talk with her."

"Did I do something wrong, Capitán?"

"Oh no, I have better plans for her. Do me a favor too, amigo."

"What is that?"

"Ease up on Ronaldo, he deserves a second chance. You of all men should know what it's like to receive one."

"But…"

"Ahh-ahh," Capitán says as he shakes his head. "Do I have to make it an order?!"

"No, Capitán, you are still appealing to a friend," he lowly replies.

"Gracias, I owe you one."

"More than one," Javier replies as he smirks.

He calmly climbs the ladder and gets on deck. He looks up to find Catalina in the ship's watchtower. She has a look of excitement as she scans the ocean's horizon through a periscope. A smile can be seen by El Capitán's view as she changes directions to watch the whales break in and out of the ocean and shoot water out of their blowholes.

"Catalina, mi amor."

"Oh Alejandro!" She says as she waves at him, "the view is so amazing!"

"I need you to come down."

"What did you say" she asks as the rough waves dampen his voice.

"I said…"

"Boom! Boom! Boom!" roars out of the cannons' mouths.

The loud noise causes Catalina to panic, while the impact tosses her forward, and she almost falls out of the tower.

"Dios Mio!" she exclaims while she manages to land a grip to stay in the tower.

Alejandro hurries to position himself underneath her in case he has to break her fall. "Por favor, mi amor. I need you to come down from there."

"No!" She replies in a bull-headed manner.

He recognizes that look and it reminds him of their adolescent years. No matter what he and his friends were up to, Catalina wanted to come along and she hated to hear that she was not able to because of her female gender.

"I need you for another task, my dear."

"It better not be cooking, Alejandro," she says.

"No, I need an instructor on Swordsmanship."

"What?" Crissino asks as he passes El Capitán with the mop. "What can she teach me?"

"Plenty, my first lessons in fencing came from her as a youth."

"You're not serious, Capitán."

"Alejandro," she says, "I see something up ahead."

"What is it?"

"I don't know, it's some sort of strange light, it's like a reflection."

she replies.

El Capitán draws out his gold-plated periscope and runs towards the front of the ship. He slowly scans the panoramic view, and slightly to his right, he sees a tiny white flag and a reflection blinds him briefly.

"I see it! Good job, Catalina! Rogelio, we have someone up ahead and they need help! Eduardo summon the rest of the crew."

Eduardo runs towards the ladder and yells, "We have someone in distress!"

The rest of the crew comes on deck to change the sail's direction to get to the small boat that is drifting in the ocean. As they sail close, they can clearly see that it's two men with a parrot on one's shoulder.

They finally get to the small roaming boat and the Chinamen Twins toss the two ropes to tie the boat and pull it out of the water and get them onto the ship.

"Thank you very much," an English gentleman says," You are most generous."

Guillermo and Otavio help them get off the boat. By the Looks of them, they can clearly see they've been floating in the Atlantic for weeks. Along with the English gentleman is some sort of Native. He wears a cloth around his waist and trinkets around his neck. The parrot flaps his wings and circumspectly flies around the ship's deck.

"My name is Capitán Alejandro De Los Amantes and I welcome you aboard 'El Amante Del Mar'."

Pablo, Edwin, Guillermo and Javier help to unload the trunk off the boat and Guillermo opens the trunk and finds a Viking horn. He grabs it and dares himself to blow it.

The native snatches it out of Guillermo's hands and the reaction causes the men to draw their weapons.

"Whoa, Whoa," says the English man as he steps in front of his native friend to protect him. "We mean no harm. I am James Galambos and this is Kike. He is from the Arawak Taino Tribe from the Island of Boriken. We are the remainders of the Protectors of the Seven Seas."

"Remainders," Guillermo asks.

"Yes, remainders," James replies.

"Lower your weapons, " El Capitán says, " Carry on Señor James."

"The Protectors of the Seven Seas help The Guardians of the New World to preserve its supernatural phenomenas. We were ambushed by an evil-English pirate that goes by the name of El Tiburón on a stop in the Virgin Islands."

"Yes, we defeated him near San Juan Bay."

"He was able to seize our vessel. He tried to force our members to submit to his command, but they chose death. Kike and I were able to hide and escape with the contents of this trunk while he sailed towards the Canary Islands."

"What's up with your compadre and that horn? " Javier asks.

"That horn will summon the Sea Creatures they call 'The Krakens'. This trunk contains all the secrets that the Seven Seas contains. We will be most indebted to you if you can kindly take us back to the Guardians on your journey to New Spain, Capitán, I've heard many great tales of your bravery, you are a famous sailor."

"Thank you for your flattery, but we ourselves are on an expedient quest and we can use experienced men to help us."

"What kind of quest does your King have you on?" James asks him.

"We no longer serve España," He replies.

"This is news to me; Spain's most heralded sailor has gone rogue?"

"The King practices two distinct forms of justice that nearly cost me my life and we have the map that leads us to the Temple of Death. We must secure its contents before the King does."

"It's contents are filled with pure evil, that is why it is called the ' Temple of Death'," James says.

"Will you help us?"

James rubs his chin in deep thought as he contemplates El Capitán's request. "You and your men are mad, but mad men make the best sailors. I have to ask you, Capitán, what are your intentions with Monteczuma's Armor? That is what you are pursuing?"

"We want to make sure no one else obtains this power. The fate of the world depends on it. Plus, we want to stick it to that unjust king of ours."

James Galambos stares deep into the eyes of each man and he goes along with his instincts because his instincts never fail him. "I will sail with you on two conditions."

"What are your conditions, Señor James?" Javier asks.

"First, you all must join our righteous establishment, and second, you must entrust me with Monteczuma's Armor to hand it over to the Guardians of the New World."

"May I ask," Guillermo says, "Who are these Guardians and why should we trust them?"

"They are a peaceful tribe from the Seminole Nation that guards the Fountain of Youth. They also help preserve the New World's many secrets. They will ensure the armor's safety. Join us for a cause greater than yourself. Join us to ward off tyranny and fight against the evil that lurks these waters!"

"I cannot speak for them," El Capitán says, "but I'm in."

"This seems muy loco." Alberto says.

This causes the men to go in shock because Alberto hardly speaks a word. Guillermo constantly jokes that his words are on a certain count and once they expire, he will as well.

"Wahh, muy loco!" The parrot cries out loud as it flaps its wings and hops around the sailors, "Wahh! Wahh! Wahh!"

"Pajaro likes rum, but rum no like Parajo," Kike says as he motions a gesture of his bird being drunk.

"They can help us," Javier says, " I'm in."

"I'm in," Edwin says.

They all agree to join the Protectors of the Seven Seas as El Capitán asks each member of the ship one by one.

"Everyone must kneel," says James as he draws out his sword, "Including you, my lady."

"She is my bride-to-be, Señor."

"Then you don't have a problem with her being a member, do you?"

"No."

"Good, the Protectors believe in equality for all genders. Women are just as viable as men."

"I couldn't agree with you more, Señor," Catalina says as she slowly kneels with the rest of them.

"I, James Galambos, an outstanding member, who has sworn to protect the Seven Seas and combat darkness wherever it dwells, asks you here today to make that very same oath. Do you swear to protect the Seven Seas?"

"We do," they all respond.

"Do you swear to fight for the liberty of the oppressed?"

"We do."

"Do you swear to assist the Guardians in preserving the supernatural phenomenas that they are entrusted with?"

"We do."

"I, James Galambos, now declares all of you to be beloved members of our righteous establishment and reveal to you our society's ancient secrets."

"Here! Here!" Guillermo exclaims, "Viva la Mar!"

"Viva la Mar!" They all yell out.

"Wahhh, Viva la Mar!" The parrot says, "Wahhh, Viva la rum!"

James reveals the "Book of Ancients" to all the members and he expounds the Protectors' history and its origin. The morale on "El Amante Del Mar" is at its highest as they continue on their quest to sail West.

***

El Capitán and his men finally reach the Yucatán Peninsula's coastline after five weeks of sailing west and doing a brief stop in San Juan for supplies.

"I see tierra up ahead," says Eduardo as he looks through his periscope from the Watchtower.

"Take a look," El Capitán says as he passes his periscope to

Catalina.

"Oh, Alejandro!"

"That is one of God's many untouched beauties."

"It is marvelous."

"Señor James," he yells.

"Yes, Capitán."

"Are you sure we should start our expedition here?"

"Yes, it will lead us to a tiny church not too far from here. I know a priest who can assist us with our journey. He is very knowledgeable of the Aztec priestly rituals."

"Listen here hombres, I want Javier, Guillermo, Rogelio, the Chinamen Twins, Ronaldo, Edwin, and my primo to come with me, Señor James, Kike, and Catalina. The rest of you will stay and guard the ship. Pablo is in charge until we return. Now, let's get to work."

It takes about forty-five minutes to gather everything and prepare the rowboats that will get them to shore.

"The ship is all yours, Pablo."

"She will be in great care, Capitán."

"That's all I ask."

The team splits in half as Rogelio, the Chinamen Twins, Guillermo, Javier, and Otavio are the first to leave the ship in the first rowboat. Kike sends his parrot up ahead in case there is peril on the peninsula's coast. The rest are on the second rowboat as they paddle their way towards the coast.

Hawks call out while they swoop towards the waters to catch

something worth eating. The jagged rocks near the beach break up the ocean's constant sending of waves that dissipate when it reaches shore. The Sun's nozzle is turned all the way up and the humidity causes their skin to be drenched from their own sweat.

El Capitán wipes his forehead with a piece of cloth and hands it to Catalina while he helps unload the boat of their supplies.

"So which way is it?" Javier asks.

"It's right this way." James replies as he shows them a narrow path up the high cliff.

"This priest," El Capitán asks, "he does know about the leyenda, am I correcto?"

"He is a descendant of Monteczuma's lineage and he was handed down this leyenda since the day of his birthright. His name is Padre Samuel Cuauahtemoc Quezada. He can help us maneuver in the temple once we get there."

They trek through the thick jungle as the Chinamen fight off the snakes they meet while making a path with their machetes. They come across a healthy stream of water that leads to a tiny village tilled with straw huts.

"The church is in the village," James says.

They can sense that the eyes of the village people are all on them as they navigate towards the Catholic Church. A few children pay them no mind while they chase each other around with tiny spears.

"This village is what remains of the Mayan Nation. Most were slaughtered by the zealous Spaniards who sought to convert the people to Christianity. Those that remained were allowed to live as long as they served the Church."

They get to the Church that is made out of cut stone. And they see that the Church is not extravagant at all. Only a wooden cross is embedded into the humble building to indicate its significance. They walk up the high steps, and near the entrance, a short priest is there to greet his visitors.

"Oh, my great amigo, Santiago Galambos, it is so great to see you. I see you have new friends, but where are the other Protectors?"

"They lost their lives, Padre Quezada."

"Oh my," Padre Quezada says, "May Dios be with them, my Son. Well, please enter, you are just in time for dinner."

"Padre, this is my friend, Capitán Alejandro De Los Amantes, his future bride Catalina and his men."

"May Christ be with you, my Son. I only ask that you respect el Casa De Dios and leave your weapons outside."

"We will kindly respect your request, Padre. Otavio, you have first watch. Ronaldo will relieve you in a couple hours."

"As you command, Capitán," Otavio says as the men lay down their weapons.

They walk into the Church and follow Padre Quezada towards the back where a section is fitted for dining. Two of his assistants prepare places for their guests and their humble staple of pozole soup is served to them.

"Uhmm," Edwin says, "You must show me how this is prepared, Padre."

"One of these days, my Son. So tell me, Capitán, what brings the King's most dauntless sailor in this part of Mexico? I have heard wondrous tales of your successful campaign at Vera Cruz. The citizens of España hold you very dear to their hearts."

"His duties no longer suits España's cause, Padre, he is now part of The Protectors."

"Is this true, Capitán?"

"Si, Padre, Señor James speaks el verdad," El Capitán replies.

"If you don't mind, would you please tell me how this came to be?"

"The King's son conspired to have me put to death for matters of el Corazón, and my men were able to rescue me before I reached the hangman's gallows."

"And your future bride, is she the razón for your unwarranted exodus?"

"Si, Padre," Catalina says. "When I discovered the prince's plot that led to Alejandro's falsely accused arrest, he locked me away and tried to rid me as well."

"So, you two have come to seek refuge in these parts?"

"No, Padre," El Capitán replies. "We are here to ask you to help us find the Secret Temple of Muerte. Señor James said you can help us on our quest."

Padre Quezada gives James a quick glance to test the temperature of the room. If El Capitán is working some type of angle to accomplish a rouse of deception, now is the time for James to indicate it. Instead, James gives him a nod of reassurance to help ease the Padre's initial worries.

"This temple contains a darkness that struck fear to the most learned Aztec Priests during their time. No one must awaken the darkness out of its deep slumber. No one has ever dared to touch this temple for centuries because no one is prepared for the release of its contents, Capitán."

"I recognize that grave consequences are heavily bound with this quest, Padre. But the King is sending men to retrieve it because he wants to possess Monteczuma's Armor and we don't have time to debate whether it's right or wrong. We need your help, now will you assist us, Padre?"

He rises from his seat and dabs his face with a piece of cloth while he says, "Follow me."

He leads El Capitán, Catalina, and James to a narrow hallway that cuts to the left near the rear section of the Church. He reaches for a thin piece of iron and uses it to leverage a large stone in the concrete floor. A tiny staircase gets revealed to the other three while Padre Quezada reaches for a candle to use as they step down to the hidden chamber.

"I have an Aztec book called 'El Libro De Jagures'. The priests used this to carry out their sacrificial ceremonies. Each enchantment has the dates of every time they were conducted."

"What is all this?" El Capitán asks as he looks around and sees shelves filled with dust, cobwebs, and books.

"This chamber is a secret library to help preserve what is left of the Ari Mayans and the Aztecs," he replies as he pulls out a wooden stool to help his short stature reach for the books on the highest shelf. He clears the cobwebs before he grips a large book made of stone. When he pulls it down, he blows on it to clear the dust that has been settled on it for years before he lays it on the table in the center of the library.

El Capitán and Catalina carefully peek over the priest's shoulders and see that the stone has two Jaguars carved into the stone facing each other. Two more candles get lit on the table to allow the priest to translate the symbols in the book.

"What kind of parchment is this?" Catalina asks.

"It is made of human skin, Señorita," he replies.

"What a savage people!" She quickly exclaims.

James and El Capitán give Catalina a sharp look to be more

sensitive of the Mestizo Priest's bloodline.

"Oh, forgive me Padre," she says as she covers her lips with embarrassment.

"It's ok Señorita, you are muy correcto. My ancestors were very barbaric in nature. They believed that sacrificing humans helped to quench their god's thirst for blood and that it would give them military and agricultural strength. It is ironico how one oppressive people can become oppressed by a people from across the ocean."

"You have razón, Padre," James says.

"Here it is."

"That's strange," James says.

"What's the problem?" El Capitán asks.

Padre Quezada begins to feel the characters and says, "It's strange because these characters have never been arranged in this manner."

"What does it say?" James asks.

"Four hundred years ago, during the building of the Aztec Capital of Tenochtitan, the mountain erupted with a volcanic blast that caused the earth to split and crack. A river of fire flowed from the mountain's mouth while large rocks spit out, destroying anything in its path.

"The priest's decided to call on the god of the inner-earth to stop his destructive outburst. Instead, evil spirits filled the atmosphere with darkened smoke and possessed the souls of five women. They drowned their children in the sacred lake and they cried black tears with terrible voices while doing so."

"Can they be defeated?" El Capitán asks.

"It does not say so here. It says that the priests were able to subdue them by calling out the enchantment in reverse and using flames. They commanded Las Lloronas to rest in the bottom of the sacred lake. They fear flames because it reminds them of their dwelling place where torment never ceases to exist."

"They sound like Demonios, Padre," Catalina says.

"Perhaps you are right, Catalina, this book is very unholy and littered with indigenous witchcraft."

"What does it say about the Armor of Monteczuma?" El Capitán asks.

"Before the Aztecs marched South to Mexico, they dwelt near what is now called Colorado. Eight hundred years ago, a very large stone from the sky hit the earth with a devastating blow. A large amount of the Aztec population suffered death. Where the stone left its imprint in the earth, very large deposits of a strange metal was left behind from the impact.

"They believed that the god of the inner-earth gave them this gift to help them conquer the land they marched on. The Aztecs forged armors and weapons out of this strange metal for their fierce Jaguar warriors. The ruler's armor was overlaid with solid gold while the rest in silver. When the entire set of armors are worn, the cosmic powers allows the captured army of the underworld to possess the souls of the armor bearers.

"With these armors, the Aztecs were able to conquer any adversary they faced on their mission to rule every place they stepped foot on. This enabled them to subject their enemies into slavery and build the temples that were required for their White god to return to them."

"So will you accompany us, Padre," El Capitán asks.

"Will you be graceful in dividing a portion of the spoils with this villita pobre?"

"Of course we will, Padre," James replies.

As they begin to leave, El Capitán holds Padre Quezada back and asks him, "Would you officiate my Matrimonio with Catalina, Padre?"

"When we regressa, my Son."

"Gracias Padre, you are most kind."

"De nada Capitán, now get some rest, we leave before the sol rises."

After six hours of sleep, they wake up and prepare for their journey to the temple before day breaks forth. Padre Quezada gathers everyone around to kneel for prayer.

"Dios, in the name of our Señor, Jesus Cristo, we pray that you watch over our every step on this journey to combat evil. We pray that you lead us with El Espiritu Santo. Amen."

"Amen," gets said as each makes the sign of the cross across their chest.

The short mestizo priest looks around and he notices that Catalina is just as prepared as the rest of them.

"Excuse me, Capitán," he says as he pulls him to the side," Is Catalina making the journey as well?"

"Yes, Padre, is that an issue?"

"This is a very dangerous trip, Capitán. Lives can be lost."

"She's more than capable of fending for herself."

"Are you sure?"

"Si, you'll see for yourself. That's what attracts me to her—her fierce bravery. Granted, stubbornness is attached to her bravery, and I'm not going to be the one who tells her she cannot come."

"If you say so, Capitán."

"Gather around men and Catalina,'" he says, "We must be careful as we make our way to the temple. Padre Quezada says there are indigenous tribes that still rebel against Espaha's sovereignty and the battle for these lands has soldiers roaming around these parts. Be on alert at all times, am I claro?"

"Si," they all reply.

"To glory!" he exclaims.

"Viva La Mar!" they all chant back.

"Wahh," the parrot crows, "Viva la rum!"

The Chinamen Twins lead the expedition as they hack a path for the rest to follow. While they make their way through the jungle, the sounds of creatures that have never been heard before ring in their ears; they stay alert to the perils that might arise.

"We must go north from here," Padre Quezada says while he helps navigate the land.

After a couple of hours of hiking in the humid jungle, they hear sounds of running footsteps shooting past them. They immediately halt when Rogelio holds his hands up when he hears a branch snap, and Kike signals everyone to be quiet.

Otavio and Edwin get a little restless and they both take a few steps backwards while they reach for their guns to prepare for battle. Their missteps causes traps to lock onto their ankles and a cargo net entraps them and carries them above the rest of the crew on a tree branch.

"Ahhhh!" they both exclaim as they fly upwards and hang on the massive tree.

The crew instantly raises their weapons while tribesmen jump out from the ground while others swoop in while swinging from trees to protect their territory. About twenty-five combatants have El Capitán and his crew surrounded.

"What should we do," Javier asks as the tribesmen take cautious steps towards them.

"You can start by getting us down," Edwin yells as he and Otavio struggle in the cargo net.

A voice from behind them causes a hole to be made to allow him to step forward. A tiny bone goes through the man's nose as he approaches El Capitán. A gold necklace hangs around his neck with different symbols and a turquoise robe hangs on his shoulders. The different patterns that are embroidered matches the iron staff that helps him maneuver through the tough terrain.

"I, Chiconcuetzali, Chief of the Tonacatecutli Tribe. You intrude the sacred land of our Lizard God. Take your men and leave."

"Perdona mi," El Capitán says, "We mean no harm."

"Why do you intrude our sacred land?"

"We are merely passing through, Chief Chiconcuetzali. We are seeking the Secret Temple of Teccistecatl," Padre Quezada replies.

The tribesmen gasp for air when they hear the temple's name and bow down.

"That temple does not exist," The Chief says, "Go and leave, do not come back or face death."

"Boom! Boom!"

Two tribesmen get shot from behind by Spaniards with musket rifles, half of the tribesmen defend themselves by attacking Spanish Infantrymen.

"Miquiztli!" yells a tribesman behind Chiconcuetzali.

"What is he saying?" El Capitán asks.

"He's saying death!" Padre Quezada exclaims.

"Rogelio and Catalina, cut down our men! The rest of you, hasta la muerte!"

"To the death!" Guillermo replies as he marches toward two tribesman.

They courageously fight off the onslaught by the tribesmen. El Capitán weaves left and right to avoid the accurately thrown spears. He then slices his way as he and his men rumble in the Yucatán jungle.

Catalina manages to release Cristobal and Edwin from the net. As they land on their feet, a spear flies past Edwin's right ear and snatches a patch of his reddish-orange hair. A bit of anger overtakes him and he fires his gun and injures an enemy.

The tribesmen push them back as the battle starts to go their way. The men try to maintain their lives while they slowly retreat towards the edge of a cliff. Padre Quezada slips and falls and a tribesman takes advantage by hopping onto him.

He moves his head to avoid a fatal blow and struggles for survival. Catalina pierces the tribesman's back with her sword. The tribesmen tactfully surround their intruders and continue to push them towards the edge of the cliff.

El Capitán makes a final surge with Rogelio's and the Chinamen's help to push the tribesmen back.

"Mizquiztli!" They chant as they continue to move towards them.

"We have to jump!" El Capitán says.

"Are you loco?!" Javier exclaims.

"It's either that," he says as he continues to fight, "or die!"

They weigh their options and they each realize that the water is always a better one, they all take a twenty-foot dive into the river.

"Ahhh! Ahhh!" Is what comes out as they make their death-defying plunge into the cold river. The current violently pushes them west. El Capitán manages to find Catalina and they hold onto each other tight while the others fight to stay afloat. They all do their best to avoid the jagged rocks embedded into the river bed.

Rogelio and Javier grasp onto a rock and they form a chain to help save the rest. The chain becomes successful as they finally get to the river's bank.

"Well," El Capitán says as he smirks and wrings out his soaked hair, "that was fun!"

"Who fired those muskets?" Ronaldo asks.

"The Governor's infantry," Rogelio replies.

"Is everyone okay?" Guillermo asks, as he goes around and checks each person individually.

"Where are we, Padre?" El Capitán asks as he wrings out his shirt.

"We are on track," he replies, " We go north from here. We still have six clicks to go."

"We will set up camp and regroup here, we will resume tomorrow."

He helps Catalina get to a secluded place to help dry off and asks, " Mi Amor, are you fine?"

"Am I fine," she exclaims, "You nearly got us killed, Alejandro!"

" I'm so…"

"I never had so much fun en mi vida!"

"Are you serious?"

"Yes, being trapped in that tiresome palace caused me to forget the jewels of adventures the world has in store," she says while she embraces him.

"You are loca!" he says as he pats her on her soaked back.

"Capitán," Javier says while he stands ten feet away.

"Si, Javier."

"May I have a word with you?"

"What is it, Amigo?"

"Did you see their eyes when padre Quezada mentioned the temple?"

"I did."

"They looked at us like we have a death wish!"

"What is new, Javier?"

"I have bad sentiments about this! We nearly died in that river! I don't like it, Capitán! I don't like it one bit!" Javier storms away after he speaks his peace. He walks away in a nervous and anxious manner while he helps everyone else set up camp.

"Is he okay?" Catalina asks.

"He'll be fine, he's just processing the situación we are in."

"Are you sure, it seems to me that he is doing more than processing. I don't want to come between your friendship with him."

"Oh no, mi Amor," He says as he brushes her damp hair to the side. "That's how we overcome our adventures. He worries while we go through el infiernno's fires, my love. He just needs some space to get his thoughts in order."

The night begins to encompass the jungle while they all get settled and eat around the camp fire. Javier's nerves calm down while he takes a sip of some dark rum that he purchased from San Juan. He passes the rum around in case there's any tension left from today's activity.

"Hoo! Hoo! Hoo!" calls out the nocturnal owl.

"Wahhh. Wahhh," Pajaro sounds off to counter the owl's call. Crickets sing as well into the still, very humid air while bats flap their wings and squeak in the open night sky.

"I have a question, Capitán," James says.

"Ask what you may, Señor James."

"Tell me the true story of Vera Cruz. I've heard so many versions of your famous campaign, I want to know how did you and your men survive the formidable English Navy?"

"Ha! Ha!" El Capitán laughs out loud as he says, "You would never believe me, Señor James."

"Please, entertain me with it."

"Do you want to tell him, Guillermo?"

"Oh no. I cannot," Guillermo replies.

"I'll tell it," Rogelio the Moor says. He takes a manly swig from the silver flask of rum to frighten the skeletons in his closet. The scars on Rogelio's face shows that his resilience is the only reason why he is able to tell this story. Everyone in the camp quiets down and the crackles of the fire is the only thing that is heard before he speaks.

"I was still new on Capitán Rodriguez's ship. Only eight months removed from surviving that slave ship headed towards the colonies. We were bringing supplies to Havana when the English made an aggressive advancement towards us. We were out shipped, four to one, and Capitán Rodriguez panicked, he froze during this intense confrontation and issued an order to surrender.

"After that day I never questioned Allah's existence. You might worship him through Jesus, and I through the Prophet Muhammed, but he exists."

"What happened next?" Padre Quezada asks as the story begins to intrigue him.

"El Capitán refused to acknowledge his Captain's orders and locked him in his quarters. With the four warships on our buttocks, Alejandro ordered us to turn back towards Vera Cruz and lighten the ship with all its unneeded cargo and supplies." He laughs after he takes another sip of rum, and continues with the story, "I can still hear the Admiral cursing El Capitán with every evil name in the Spanish language."

The rest of the men who were there laughed as well.

"We were able to sail very fast towards Vera Cruz. It gave us three hours to defend the Mexican harbor. El Capitán was able to convince the other captains to sink their own ships to barricade the English in a trap. The brutish English sailed right into it and suffered defeat."

"A lot of honorable men died that night," El Capitán says as he holds Catalina tightly. "That was el dia that I realized that one must be willing to die for his beliefs in order to live."

"To the fallen at Vera Cruz," Guillermo says.

"To the fallen," the rest say.

"There's no better group of men that I would rather die for," El Capitán says as he takes a sip from the flask.

75

"I hate to break up this touching momento, Muchachos," Padre Quezada says, "But we must get our rest, we have a long day ahead of us mañana."

***

Just before the sun rises from the east, they resume their journey to locate the temple. As usual, the Chinamen Twins continue to hack their way through for the next four hours.

Tuyen takes a swing of his machete and he hits a rock-like surface and the vibration tweaks his wrist a bit.

"Ahh." he says.

"What's wrong, Tuyen?" Pho asks.

"Take a look." he replies as he taps the stone wall again.

"We should be here," Padre Quezada says, as he checks the map.

The neglected stone walls are covered with moss and plant life. Everyone examines the wall while they rip off branches and vines to expose the concrete. The stone gives more of an appearance of an old mausoleum than it does a temple filled with gold.

"It's only six feet high, the temple should be much larger," El Capitán says.

"I knew this was all a rouse," Edwin says.

"This can't be," El Capitán says, as he shakes his head.

El Capitán is confused, he tries to find a secret entrance by scanning the walls made of stone. Each wall is six by six. He grabs the map and takes a look at it as he leans against a tree. He puts down his gear and wipes the sweaty frustration off his forehead.

"Something—" he tries to say before he slips and falls while a branch of the tree bends and causes the ground beneath them to shake. Just to the left of where El Capitán is, a shaft opens and it reveals a makeshift staircase.

"Our treasure awaits us, Amigos!" he exclaims as he jumps on his feet and dusts himself off.

El Capitán is the first to walk down the staircase. He grabs a torch and lights it up and encourages them to follow him.

"Stand close to me, Catalina."

The temple releases a rancid mildew stench while water drips down from the ceiling of the stairs. The narrow stairway goes down twenty feet before they reach the temple's ground floor.

The bottom floor is flooded about six inches high and James lights up two more torches and hands one to Javier. Padre Quezada walks up towards the wall and signals for Javier to give him some light to read the Aztec symbols.

"What does it say, Padre?" Javier asks.

"Welcome to the Temple of Muerte," he replies.

Javier's stomach turns when he becomes overwhelmed with fear while a loud shriek echos in the temple's halls, and a grayish streak passes them by in a quick flash. The light to the torches goes out and they are surrounded by complete darkness.

"What was that?!" Ronaldo asks in a frantic tone.

The temple becomes very quiet while James and Javier try to re-light the torches. The only thing that can be heard are the tiny drops of water hitting the flooded floor. Another shriek echoes in the hallway, but this time it is amplified even louder. Everyone covers their ears to protect them from the evil screech.

"It's Las Lloronas," Guillermo exclaims.

Climbing the side of the walls and the ceiling are live grayish beings with water dripping from their bodies. They make their way towards them and attack.

"Dios mio!" Padre Quezada says as he mumbles a prayer after signing the cross with his fingers.

"Boom! Boom!"

Rogelio and Edwin fire their weapons and it does nothing to stop Las Lloronas assault. Two leap off the right wall and jump on Guillermo and Kike while the other three ram into Rogelio, Javier, and El Capitán to show their supernatural strength.

Catalina comes to her fiancé's rescue and inserts her sword into the gray being's back. The evil creature twists her neck and stares at Catalina with her entirely black eyes. She lets out a loud shriek as dark tears flow down her face while she spits black water out of her mouth.

This causes Catalina to get disgusted while she tries to make out what she is drenched with. The evil creature swats her left hand at Catalina and it causes her to hit the wall very hard.

"No!" El Capitán yells as he slices the creature's head off.

The head falls to the ground and shrieks in anger while the body continues towards Catalina.

"Padre!" James says as he tries to help Kike maintain his life, "We need your help!"

Padre grabs a torch. takes a swig of Holy oi,l and he spits it through the flames to light up the headless creature attacking Catalina.

"En el nombre De Jesus Cristo!" he exclaims.

"Rahhhh!" The dismembered head screeches, and the spirit leaves.

El Capitán goes to help the rest of the men as Padre Quezada waves the torch and does the same to two more creatures.

"Rahhh! Rahhh!"

The other two back up in fear while they watch their companions get taken out.

"This is not over, Capitán!" The one on the left says in a demonic voice, "We will find you and destroy you!"

Padre Quezada tries to coat them with fire, but when he does so, they leap to the side, hop on the ceiling, and try to escape the temple. In his second effort he sets one on fire.

"En el nombre De Jesus Cristo!"

"Rahhhh! Rahhh! We will find you!" It says as the dark spirit vanishes and gets sent back to its fiery eternal dungeon of imprisonment.

El Capitán helps Catalina get up while everyone tries to make sense of everything that just went down in that temple.

"Did you get them all, Padre?" James asks.

"All but one, my Son; she escaped into the jungle."

"Are you okay, Catalina?"

"I bumped my head and she spewed some sort of putrid water on me," she replies while she tries to rub out the pain.

"There, there, mi amor," he says as he kisses the bump on her head.

"Is everyone okay?" Javier asks. "Let me look at that Guillermo."

Guillermo's arm has some serious claw marks that goes from his shoulder to across this chest.

"I'm fine," Guillermo says as he pulls his arm away from Javier and winces at the same time.

"You are not fine, let me see it."

"She clawed me good."

Padre Quezada rubs Holy Oil over Guillermo's wounds and says a prayer. He heats up a steel rod that he pulled from his bag with the torch and he presses it on the wounds to seal it and keep it from worsening.

"Ahhh. Padre! That's not Christ like!"

"May God heal you, my Son."

"Okay, now Padre," El Capitán says, "Please lead the way."

"We must be very careful, the Aztec priests were very meticulous when it comes to laying out their traps to keep intruders out."

They cautiously go through a web of corridors that was purposely made like a confusing maze as Padre Quezada leads them. It almost resembles the Aztec Calendar if the blueprints of the temple is shown to them. The Padre's carefulness successfully leads them to a door and he checks for any traps when he approaches it. He reads the symbols and he shakes his head as he does so.

"What is it, Padre?" Catalina asks.

"This stone opens the door, but it seems too easy."

He decides to push the stone in while everyone expects the worse to happen. The walls give a light tremble as the door slides open, and it gives everyone a sigh of relief when nothing else happens. They go through the narrow corridor, and half way in, the door behind them shuts very fast while the floor shakes, and large swinging blades swoop from both sides near their feet.

"Look out below," El Capitán says while he hops out of the way while everyone follows suit.

Everyone is able to clear the hurdle, but another set of blades that are aiming towards their heads swings out. Javier pulls down Alejandro while everyone else notices it and ducks out of the way. The tiny delay of El Capitán causes his hat to suffer the demise intended for him. As they all stand, another blade from the top gets released and Ronaldo pushes Rogelio to the side to save him from being split in two.

"Ay. Dios Mio!" El Capitán exclaims as he checks himself.

"Are you okay. Alejandro?" Catalina asks as she checks for herself.

"I'm fine, mi amor, it was my favorite Gorra that paid the price."

Ronaldo gives Rogelio a hand to help him up.

"Gracias, Ronaldo, you saved my life."

"I'm sure you'll do the same when it presents itself."

"We must continue to move forward, my Children," padre Quezada says. He walks up to the second door and he pushes with all his might to lodge open the door. Javier and Kike help to give the Mestizo priest momentum and they accomplish the task of opening it. They can sense it is a large space, but the vast amount of darkness doesn't allow them to see the size of the chamber.

Javier steps in and he hears the sound of pouring water and a tiny dripping sound as well. Kike sticks his hand out towards the wall to find a torch, and instead, he feels a weak stream dripping into a reservoir. He feels the liquid and sniffs the tip of his fingers. The liquid smells like crude oil and he strikes a match to light up the reservoir. The oil sparks up and a trail begins to take place as the entire room lights up in a matter of seconds.

"Empty," Guillermo says with disappointment, "There's nothing here but a stupid fountain!"

The fountain is made out of sterling silver. The water gushing from it is the reason the temple is flooded. El Capitán and Catalina walk towards it in confusion.

"Once again," Javier says, "We risk our lives for a fable. We've come away empty, Capitán."

"Now is not the time to be so bathetic, Javier!"

"Look Alejandro," Catalina says as she points to the bottom of the fountain, "What is this?"

She pulls out a shiny piece of metal and all the water escapes down its drain. The water to the fountain stops flowing and the temple shakes very violently. The dust from the loosened walls covers everyone while the large wall in front of them comes crashing down.

Everyone does their best to hold on to whatever is still fastened to the temple to help them endure the tremors. Once the shaking stops, and all the dust settles, they see a light shine forth from the torn wall.

"Uhh-huh-huh," El Capitán is coughing and trying to wave the dust from his face.

"Look, Capitán!" Otavio says in excitement.

"What is it, Primo?"

"We found the treasure! " Guillermo says with his mouth left open in amazement.

There are piles and piles of gold coins, rubies and emerald gems. In the center are twenty silver armors and the golden armor hangs over them. The Armor has a shine on it that entices one to sport it's magnificence in the time of battle.

"Wow!" Comes out of Catalina's mouth as she touches the Aztec trinkets made of gold.

"This treasure is more than I ever imagined," Guillermo says.

***

It took the men two weeks to secure every piece of gold and gem out of the temple. The top of the temple was a shaft to initially help the Aztec's transport their coveted treasure. The gold was enough to make everyone in the village and on the ship rich.

Padre Quezada took the silver armors and entrusted the men of his village to hide them all over the Southern region of Mexico to never be found by those who seek its evil power.

Just before they sail towards the Floridian Everglades, El Capitán finally finds the time to wed his lovely bride.

"Alejandro De Los Amantes, do you lawfully take Catalina Beatriz Delgado to be your wife in sickness and in health?"

"Si, padre."

"Catalina Beatriz, do you take Alejandro De Los Amantes to be your husband in sickness and in health?"

"Si, Padre."

"In the name of Christ, I pronounce you Esposo y Esposa. You may kiss the bride."

The entire crowd in attendance claps and chants while the two passionately lock lips while embracing each other.

Pablo rushes into the church in disorientation as he tries to secure his eye patch in its proper place while breathing heavily. "Capitán!" he exclaims as he interrupts the celebration.

"What is it, Pablo?"

"They are here, Capitán! They have finally arrived!"

The Fountain of Youth

Search into the depths of the heart of any man and there will be the desire to be immortal. The Guardians of the New World have been tasked with the duty to defend this secret portal. El Capitán and his men sail on to discover the best kept mystery in America—the one Ponce Deleon could never untwine. It's the Fountain of Youth, and it is here, that ceases to exist the misfortunes of never having enough time…

Pahlo is standing in the center of the humble chapel still grasping for air to warn every one of the danger that is soon coming to the indigenous village.

"We must hurry, Capitán! There are Soldados headed this way!"

El Capitán glances at Padre Quezada while he still holds Catalina in his arms.

"Go Capitán! We will do our best to slow them down!"

"And my familia?"

"The Bishop of Seville owes me a favor; they will be out of the King's grasp soon. But you must hurry!"

"Gracias Padre," Catalina says as she hugs him.

"Go! Go!" he says, "Never surrender my children, and may Christ be with you in your righteous endeavors!"

Rogelio hands Pablo, Guillermo, Javier, Otavio and Ronaldo muskets in case a stand must be had before they reach their ship.

"We are ready, Capitán." Javier says.

"Then let's go!" he replies.

They take the shortened trail that was made for a hastened escape in case a time like this would arrive.

Catalina rips the wedding dress that was handcrafted by the village women so she can run faster. They rush past the rustling branches while trying to reach the secluded, jagged beach.

"Over here!" A soldier exclaims.

"Bang! Bang!"

They all duck for cover as bullets fly with a piercing sound past their ears. The sound of marching feet are heard from about a few hundred yards away while they get closer to the rowboat.

"Bang! Bang! Bang!"

"Ahh!" Javier exclaims as he feels a searing heat pinch the triceps to his right arm!

"Bang! Bang! Bang!"

The men fire back to buy some time as they approach the edges of the beach. Rogelio lights up a couple of sticks of dynamite while Guillermo fires a flare to signal the ship the peril they're in.

"Let's go!" El Capitán says before he fires his weapon.

"Bang!"

They all toss their weapons in the boat and push it out to sea while Catalina hops in to secure the paddles to get ready to roll.

James and Kike are watching everything take place with periscopes on the ship.

"Men," James says, "We have trouble on land, man the cannons!"

Tuyen, Pho. Alberto, and Crissino quickly head down to the cannon deck to help their shipmates get back on board safely. Cristobal gets in position on the top deck to help the men below aim the cannons perfectly.

Meanwhile, on the beach, the infantry's Sergeant is positioning the men to make another attempt to apprehend their fugitive suspects on the fleeing rowboat.

"Avanza! Avanza! They are getting away, hombres!"

"Thirty degrees up and ten degrees left." Cristobal yells while he watches the Governor's soldiers get in attack formation on the beach.

"Ready at will!" Eduardo says as he relays the message from the men below deck.

"Steady! Steady! Fire!"

The sergeant raises his hand and is about to command his men to fire when a loud blast of simultaneous thunder rips through the sunny sky.

"Boom! Boom! Boom!"

In the sky are three screeching projectiles headed their way to wreak havoc on the beach.

"Retreat!" he says while the cannonballs continue to screech towards them.

Fire, sand, and rocks burst in the air. The cannonballs explode when they hit the beach and it causes the infantrymen to surrender their apprehension of El Capitán and his rebellious band of misfits.

"Yeahhh!" exclaims El Capitán, Catalina, and the men on the rowboat while they paddle faster to get back to their humble abode.

"We are not out of trouble yet," James says as he tosses a rope to help Edwin draw up the rowboat.

"What is it?" El Capitán asks while he climbs onboard.

"We have three ships headed toward us from the north, they are two clicks away," he replies as he does his part to pull them up.

"We need help!" Edwin exclaims to get Eduardo, Kike, Cristobal, and Alberto to help while the others prepare the ship to make an escape.

"Great job men!" El Capitán says as he helps Catalina and Javier get out of the boat. "We can sail east, it will give us a better chance to be away from land to defeat them."

"I don't think so." Rogelio says while he points towards the right, "We have company in that direction!"

"Ready the cannons!" Javier says while Guillermo does a hasty job of bandaging his flesh wound.

In the center of the three-ship formation from the north is Admiral Rodriguez orchestrating the strategic approach with Epifañio and the spoiled Prince. The Admiral gets overwhelmed with joy as he watches El Capitán fall into his long-awaited trap. It took him weeks of sleepless planning to come up with a perfect stratagem to get El Capitán to sprawl in defeat.

"I finally got him, Epifañio! There he lies like a ratón caught in a cheese trap!"

"Your plan proved to be infallible and effective!" says Epifañio.

"Do not kill the girl," says the Prince.

"That is not up to us, that is up to them, Your Majesty. They have to decide whether to surrender with dignity or die as perros."

"You know him, what will he do?"

"I don't think he will do a foolish thing, he has no way out. He is pinned towards the coast."

As Spain's Naval Fleet continues to advance towards them, El Capitán tries his best to remain calm and gets overtaken with a sense of Déjà vu being played out in front of him.

"This is the sueñó,'' he lowly says to himself.

"I have a plan," James says as he rushes to the "Chest of Secrets".

"Good," El Capitán says, "We cannot surrender—El Mundo's existence depends on it!"

"Fire the cannons," Javier says as he gets the signal to do so by El Capitán.

"Boom! Boom! Boom! Boom!"

They fire the cannons towards the east and do minor damage to the ships that keep approaching them. The ship on Admiral Rodriguez's left turns the ship to get into a position to show they mean business.

"Boom! Boom!"

"Incoming!" Rogelio exclaims.

A piercing screech heads their way, it makes an uninvited crash on the deck and causes everyone to scatter. One of the ship's mast splinters in half and falls on Edwin's back.

"Voo-Vooommm!" Sounds out towards the ocean's horizon while James blows his lungs into the Norse-like horn.

"Voo-Vooommm! Voo-Vooommm!"

"What is he doing?" Pablo asks in confusion.

"He is summoning the Kraken," Guillermo replies, "Blow harder! Perhaps they are in a deep slumber!"

"Voo-Vooommm!"

"Surrender, De Los Amantes, and I will spare the lives of Catalina and your men," says the Prince through a makeshift megaphone as they get closer.

El Capitán turns towards his crew and they all see an expression on his face that they have never seen before, not even sailing towards Vera Cruz. They see an expression of defeat and hopelessness as he senses that his demise is taking place before him. He takes a look at Catalina as she tries her best to pry Edwin out from underneath the massive cracked beam. He stares at James as James stands in perplexion while still holding onto the Viking horn. Javier shakes his head in ultimate resilience to reassure El Capitán that this cause is worth dying for.

"Hasta la Muerte!" El Capitán yells as he raises his hand with his sword to the sky.

"Fire the cannons!" exclaims Javier as he waves his sword .

Admiral Rodriguez shuts his periscope in anger and yells out with spit coming out of his mouth, "You fools! Sink that ship, Capitán Vargas!"

"Ay-Ay, Admiral." the captain replies, as he relays the orders with his right hand.

"Rarrrr!" bellies out from the ocean while large waves form while a vicious tentacle crushes a ship from the east.

"It's the Kraken!" Otavio exclaims.

"Look," Eduardo says as he points, "there's another one!"

"Rarrrr!" The second one crushes the ship to the left of Admiral Rodriguez.

"No," Guillermo says, "There are three!"

The third Kraken raises a ship and splits it like a feeble twig as it towers more than forty feet over the ocean.

"Boom! Boom! Boom! Boom! Boom!" erupts from the two remaining vessels of the fleet.

"Rarrrr!" says the second Kraken while it endures a direct hit by the Admiral's lead ship.

The other two Krakens get infuriated as their companion slowly sinks into the ocean in defeat. They swoop in and head towards the two warships.

"We await your orders, Admiral!" Capitán Vargas exclaims while he sees the two beastly sea creatures come headstrong.

The Admiral is awestruck with his mouth gaping open, he watches the sea monsters tear through his fleet like paper. He remains silent while the remaining sailors think that it it's best to jump overboard.

"Abandon ship! Abandon ship!!" the Captain yells as he dives into the water.

"Rarrrrr!" the larger of the two Krakens growls out while it stares down at the Admiral as it cocks back its fierce tentacles and unleashes his wrath on the vessel.

The men on "Amante De Mar" go wild as they witness the creatures demolish their adversaries.

"Voo-Vooommm!"

James blows the horn to get their attention, the Krakens turn towards him and wink while they vanish deep into the Atlantic and await the call for help whenever it's needed.

Tiny and large pieces of wood litter the coastline while sailors are trying to survive the onslaught they just witnessed. El Capitán and his men take off and leave towards their next destination.

"Where to, Capitán?" Rogelio asks as he steers the ship northeast.

"Where do those Guardians dwell, Señor James?" El Capitán asks while his heart comes down to a normal heartbeat.

"The Floridian Everglades, Capitán," he replies.

"Señor James will guide you, Rogelio. Great job men! Dios

continues to be with us! To glory!"

"To glory!" they all exclaim.

Catalina embraces him and says. "We have unfinished business to attend to, Alejandro."

"Indeed we do, mi amor."

"Javier," she calls out loud his way.

"Si, Señora Catalina."

"You have command of the ship, El Capitán has to fulfill the duty of a husband."

The crew cheers and whistles for their heralded captain to consummate the vows of his matrimony.

"As you command, Señora Catalina," he says and bows his head and tips his hat. "You heard Señora Catalina! We sail towards Florida! Our destiny awaits us!"

"Viva la Mar!" they reply.

"Wahh, Viva la Mar!" the parrot says while it flaps with joy, "Wahhh, Viva la rum!"

El Capitán picks up his bride and he carries her over the threshold into his quarters. The men continue to celebrate and cheer while they make their way to find the Guardians of the New World.

***

Eight days into their journey, Alejandro is sitting on the edge of the bed late in the night. Catalina senses that she is sleeping alone and opens her eyes. She sees that her husband is not laying besides her.

"There you are." she says when she sits up and finds him, "come back to bed, Alejandro."

"I can't sleep."

She makes her way towards him and gently wraps her arms around him to slowly massage his shoulder blades while she kisses him.

"What troubles you?"

"Here I am, a man with everything I ever dreamed of and I cannot return home and share it with my father and Madre. I miss them, and I miss the simple life in Seville."

"So you miss the times we couldn't be together."

"Those were the days, mi amor," he says as he tickles her.

"No!" she says while she laughs and shakes her head. She fights to defend herself from the ticklish assault. "No, Alejandro!"

"So please tell me, what happened to you that noche? I waited for you and you never showed up."

"Your father never told you? Wait, you were there?"

"Yes, I was there. He discovered our plans to leave, but he still escorted me to the pier. I waited and waited, but you never appeared."

"Your father had Pedro and two more of his servants beat me to a pulp."

"He what?!"

"Yes. I know you and your father are close, but he discovered our plans and intervened. Guillermo saved me from a serious and almost catastrophic injury. He took me in and helped me heal—both my body and mi broken Corazón."

"He led me to believe that you backed out and convinced me to stay at the Royal Palace."

"I heard the news a few years later, but I figured it was muy tarde to pursue you again."

"I never stopped loving you. Is that why your mother was very coy and speaking in hidden messages?"

"What did she say?" he asks.

"She said, 'my son is not the person people want you to believe he is. One day, destiny will find its way back to you and reveal its plan.'"

"Sounds like her."

"I missed them too."

"You do?"

"Si, they always found a way to make you uncomfortable or feel embarrassed."

"That's the thing, Catalina, I feel so ashamed of how I acted towards my father. I was childish and very selfish, he only sought what was best for me. I only did everything in my power to neglect his wishes to forge my own path to be great. For what? The greatness I sought has gone up in flames! I am no better than the English pirates that I loathe so much!"

"Oh Alejandro, don't say that!" she says as she kisses him, "You are great and soon we will be reunited with them as we begin our own familia."

"What do you mean, mi amor? Are you trying to…?"

"Yes, Alejandro, I'm with child!" she says in joy while she nods excessively.

"Oh," he says, "this is great! We are going to have a baby!"

A knock on the door interrupts their great news. El Capitán goes to answer the door and he finds Javier standing there.

"We are approaching land, Capitán."

"Give me a minute, compadre."

He closes the door and he and Catalina get dressed to report to deck. He plants a kiss on her forehead before they leave the cabin. The crew is in a hurry, they maneuver the sails to slow the ship down before they hit the anchor. Along with the swamp terrain are tiny canoes filled with Seminole warriors.

"Drop the anchor," says Señor James, "we don't want to get the ship stuck in the swamp."

"Drop the anchor!" Guillermo says to Crissino and Cristobal.

The canoes make their way and James tosses a rope ladder to allow them onboard the ship. Four Seminoles get onboard before their chief steps onto the ship. The Seminoles have on simple native wear with their signature moccasins to get them through the marshy terrain. The Chief wears a necklace with charms that represent his experience as a native warrior to his tribe.

"Wahhh, wahhh, Seminoles!" the parrot says as he recognizes the guests on the ship, "Wahhh, Seminoles have good rum!"

"Pajaro," Kike says, "no more rum!"

"Wahhh, Pajaro wants rum! Wahhh, Pajaro wants rum!"

"You must do something with that crazy bird, Kike," the Chief says while he greets his two friends. "Why you two on Spanish boat?"

"It's a long story, Darkened Moon. I want you to meet my new friend, Capitán Alejandro De Los Amantes. Capitán, this is Chief Darkened moon, leader of the Guardians."

"How?"

"Buenos Dias, Señor Darkened Moon."

"Where's your other friends, James."

"They did not make it, El Tiburón killed them."

"Captain Short foot?"

"Only Kike and I survived the attack, Darkened Moon."'

"News makes me sad."

"As it does I, but El Capitán has joined our ranks and we have something you must see."

"What do you have, old friend?"

Kike helps Guillermo and Rogelio bring the heavy chest to the center of the top deck. The Seminoles that stand behind Darkened Moon show their anxiousness while El Capitán slowly opens the chest. A golden light escapes and captivates their attention while they peek at its contents.

The Chief gets blinded by the light in a brief moment and he blocks the light from continuing to do so.

"Monteczuma," escapes the mouth of one of the Seminoles and they all bow down to its beauty.

"Where did you find this armor?" Darkened Moon asks.

"We found it in the Secret Temple of Death," El Capitán replies, "It was nestled in the heart of the Yucatán's jungle."

"This armor harnesses the power of the cosmos. This metal that comes from the fallen sky only seeks to destroy the earth and its creation. No one can wear this armor."

"That's why we brought it to you," James says as he closes the chest shut.

"Do you understand its cosmic powers?" El Capitán asks.

"Man will never understand the armor's powers, the bearer will have the ability to conquer and destroy any place his feet land, but his inner-man will dissipate."

"What is one's inner-man?" Catalina asks.

"It is the goodness within all of us that guides our souls," Darkened Moon replies.

"James says you know what to do with it. You can destroy it, right?" Guillermo says.

"No, this metal is indestructible. I have a place for it. We leave tomorrow to secure it, but today we welcome you to our village."

The entire crew leaves the ship and follows the Seminoles up a river that leads them through the marshy Everglade lands. The hiss of snakes and the snaps of alligator jaws causes everyone to be on high alert as they row their way towards the village.

Twenty minutes of going east inland, the Seminoles in the lead of the pack signal that they have arrived to El Capitán and his crew. They pull the rowboats to the left side of the river bank and follow their travel guides through the thick-green, mushy trees. Tiny huts show as they continue to walk. Small trails of smoke rise as the women tend to their duties to keep the village in working order.

"So please tell me, Darkened Moon." Guillermo asks, "Does the Fountain of Youth exist?"

"Yes," he replies.

"Have you seen it with your own eyes?"

"I have both seen it and drank from it."

"Does it grant immortality?"

"No, my friend, it only extends the natural life of a man. It gives man a thousand new moons when he tastes the fountain's water."

"Will you show me this coveted place?"

"We will go tomorrow."

An infant child walks up to Catalina and hands her a necklace made of sea shells to welcome their visitors with a good gesture sign. Catalina pulls out a ruby gem to kindly return the welcoming gesture to the sweet Seminole girl. The little girl smiles and runs to stand behind her mother's leg in a shy manner and peeks back towards Catalina.

Darkened Moon speaks to his people in their native tongue to announce their guests and the purpose for their arrival. He signals to El Capitán to show forth the chest and reveal what it contains. Edwin and Pablo volunteer to expose the armor to everyone in the village. The crowd holds their breath as they gaze upon the Aztec's most prized jewel. Its presence causes quite a stir and the eldest of the village passes out in shock.

Darkened Moon catches the Medicine Man before he hits himself on the head. He tries to get him to regain conscious by patting his left cheek softly. Two tribesmen come with a bucket of water and splash it on his face. The water gets the elder tribesman to open his eyes in a dramatic fashion. His eyes roll back and he mumbles in his native tongue.

"I," he then says, "Healing Waters, has seen the death that threatens us! Death by sharp teeth soon will come for us!"

"What does he mean?" Pho asks.

"Take him away," says Darkened Moon.

Two Seminoles carry him to his hut and try their best to refrain him and calm him down. The sight of Monteczuma's Armor has driven him to the brink of insanity as he continues to utter incomplete phrases in his native tongue.

"Forgive Healing Waters, he has never uttered a prophesy such as this before. Healing Waters is very old and probably his Seminole mind is the first to leave us."

"Will he be okay?" El Capitán asks.

"Time is the only thing that solves the questions to many mysteries. Healing Waters' mystery is one that needs time. Now come, sit and break bread with us. We must begin the ceremony."

"What ceremony?" Javier asks.

"Now that you are Protectors," James whispers in his ear, "You must make an allegiance to the Guardians."

They all sit around the village's meeting circle fire. Drums beat as the bonfire gets lit to commence the ceremony. Men and women dance around the fire and the guests enjoy the entertainment while a bowl of a strange-tasting liquid gets passed around to them. El Capitán is the first to sip the liquid. He tries his best to be respectful and not gag as he holds it in with a tight fist against his mouth. Everyone else coughs while they each taste it.

"What is it?" El Capitán asks as he leans in towards James.

"It is the sweat off a toad's back." James replies.

"What?!"

The men and women of the village toss cloth bags into the fire and it causes large flames to shoot upwards with vague images as the crew begins to hallucinate from the toad's sweat. Each image depicts a story and Darkened Moon writes each one down. The first image is a ship, and then a storm pops up. The next image is a cave littered with frogs and then a distinct multitude. Each member reacts to the toad's sweat differently as the effects kick in stronger. Ronaldo is holding his stomach as he laughs uncontrollably. El Capitán is trying his best to fight it and shakes his head. Catalina hides behind her husband in paranoia while Javier draws his weapon to ward off the demons that playfully taunt him.

"Do you see them? Javier asks out loud.

"1 cannot see them," Guillermo replies, "but I can hear those demonios! They're everywhere!"

"Where are they?!" Rogelio says as he swings his sword in the air.

Kike and James fix their attention on the story being told by the flames. Their encounter with El Capitán is being confirmed by the Seminole bonfire. El Capitán is the key to manifest their own destiny.

"Do you see that Kike?" James asks.

"Yes, I see, the time has arrived," Kike replies.

After thirty minutes of facing their deepest and darkest fears, El Capitán, Catalina and the men pass out and crash for the rest of the day and the night.

***

"Capitán," James says in a low voice while nudging El Capitán to help awaken him out of his comatose state.

He opens his eyes and he's clueless as to how he and Catalina are laying in a tee-pee. He shakes his head as he clears the gook out of the corner of his eyelids. He then nudges his wife to wake up as well.

"Who put us in here?"

"Kike and I, come on, it's time to go."

"How long were we out?"

"It's a new day, Capitán."

"Remind me never to drink the sweat off a toad's back ever again," he says as he gently shakes Catalina. "Give us some time to straighten up, Señor James."

"Will do, Capitán."

Catalina and El Capitán get out of their tee-pee and they see the rest of the men trying to combat the wooziness that still lingers from the day before.

"How are you Amigo?" El Capitán asks Guillermo.

"Oooh," he replies as he receives a pat on the back. "I'm a bit groggy and mi esparda is killing me."

"The treasures of experience come with plenty of back pain," El Capitán says as he chuckles.

"God can take it all back, Capitán."

Twelve of Darkened Moon's finest warriors prepare to make the journey of securing the armor with them.

"Where are you taking us?" Javier asks as he sips from a mug of hot liquid to help rejuvenate his equilibrium.

"We will leave to the Fountain of Youth to secure the Aztec armor," Darkened Moon replies.

Darkened Moon walks behind the newlyweds while they trek the beaten path into Florida's heartland.

"How far is it?"

"Half a Sun's walk, Capitán." he replies. "We have waited many moons for your arrival."

"Is that so? Why is my arrival so important?"

"You and your men have been chosen to free a lost people."

"A lost people? What people?"

" The Tainos," he replies, as he points towards Kike.

"The Tainos have been wiped away from existence. Kike is the only Taino left."

"He's not. They exist in a different world, a world that is unknown. Your people, the Spaniards, forced Tainos to flee to that world. You are destined to bring them back. The flames spoke to me and the flames are never wrong when they speak."

"What is he talking about?" Catalina asks as Darkened Moon maneuvers past them to get to the front of the pack.

"Yo no se, mi amor. Perhaps, he had a bit of that Toad's Sweat before we left."

"That makes sense," she says as she chuckles at her husband's joke.

"How much farther must we hike?" Guillermo asks James as he tries to fight off the back pain.

"Not too much, compadre."

"When are we going to tell them?" Catalina asks.

"Tell us what?" Javier asks.

"Nothing." he replies as he stares down Catalina to keep quiet.

"We are here," Darkened Moon says as they approach a dry lake bed.

"This is it?" El Capitán says, "It seems to me that someone drank all of its agua, Chief Darkened Moon."

Chief Darkened Moon walks to the center of the lake bed as his men stand in marked out spots to form a circle around him.

"What is he doing?" Edwin asks.

"Just watch," Kike replies as he signals him to be quiet while the Seminoles summon up the fountain.

"We, Guardians of the New World, call upon you nurturing fountain to reveal yourself!" Darkened Moon yells out loud while his men stomp their sticks and feet on the dry ground.

The earth trembles and shakes while it cracks and water shoots out to fills up the dry lakebed. To the north end of the lake, the cliff twists while rocks fall into the water and it reveals an opening.

El Capitán, Catalina, and the rest of the crew stand at the edge of the lakebed in amazement. The sun shines ten times brighter at the cliff's entrance. A sparkling waterfall cascades over the cliff and a rainbow flutters as the sun continues to shed its light.

"Take the armor with you and go through the entrance, Capitán," James says, "Go and extend your natural life."

They all take a brief moment to glance at each other before they step forward. Although neither of them can make any sense of what their eyes are computing to their minds, they all decide to step forward to see what lies ahead of them. El Capitán, Catalina, and Javier are the first to enter the dark cave. Javier lights up an old torch and clears the old and dusty cobwebs while the rest slowly walk in.

"Why did they stay behind?" Otavio asks.

"You are only allowed to enter the fountain once," Guillermo replies.

A swift breeze blows out the torch and a ball of light reveals itself. The rocks shuts the opening and enclose them in. The Twins swing their swords at the glowing globe that hovers a little bit above them, but they miss as the globe easily dodges their advances. The globe pulses and releases a big flash. Everyone tries to block out the pulse with their hands to keep it from blinding their vision. As the entrance closes shut, the wall in front of them crumbles and magically forms into steps. The glowing globe stops pulsating and it follows the path.

"It wants us to follow it," El Capitán says.

"They call it the Glowing Globe of Destiny," Guillermo whispers as he lightly steps forward very slowly, "The leyenda says that this globe knows the destiny of all that faces it."

"Por favor, Guillermo!" Pablo exclaims as he nudges him, "enough with your leyendas!"

"Fine!" Guillermo says as he shows a moment of exasperation with his arms hitting his sides, "I'll just let you see for yourself!"

"Enough!" Rogelio says. "The two of you have to pull yourselves together!"

The passage comes to an end and the globe continues to hover in one place and reveals the cave's crown jewel. The water can be heard splashing as they draw close to the fountain. The fountain is decorated with assorted gems in a neat and orderly fashion while bright fluorescent blue water spills out into a tiny pool that can fit one person for bathing. The glowing globe unites with a hovering spirit as it pulses like a calm heartbeat.

"What are you?" he asks.

"I am the Spirit of Light and everything that is good. 1 am also called the Glowing Globe of Destiny. Thou and thy men have been chosen, Capitán."

"Chosen for what?"

"The light within thee is pure and thine destiny awaits thee to liberate an oppressed people. You must fight the evil that lurks these waters in these two distinct worlds—the known and the unknown."

"I do not understand your riddles, please explain them to me."

"Please step forward and drink, Capitán. Soon, these riddles will be made very clear."

El Capitán steps forward and lowers his hand to drink out of the fountain. The fluorescent water cools his throat as it slowly goes down and the cold water tingles his entire body. A strong jolt shoots through his body like lightning and he begins to glow.

"What is it?" he asks as they all stare at him.

"Look at yourself," replies Catalina.

He raises his hand and sees it glowing and pulsing at the same time while the tingle continues to run through his body. Everybody else takes their turn to drink from the fountain and they get to experience the same sensation that their captain is going through. Otavio and Eduardo are the last two to drink from it while the spirit continues to hover over them.

"Each of you now has two thousand more new moons added to your natural lives. Now, where is the Armor of Monteczuma?"

"It's right here," Javier replies.

"Please leave the armor here, it will be safely kept. Now go, your destiny awaits you and your glory will soon precede you."

The Glowing Globe of Destiny vanishes and the water from the fountain slowly stops until not a drop is left. On the wall, there are some hooks in place and El Capitán decides to hang the shiny, golden armor on them. Javier lights up the torch again and they walk back towards the entrance. When they get to the entrance, the rocks open up and allows them to exit the Fountain of Youth. Standing outside of the cave is James, Kike, and the Seminoles waiting for them to return.

"That was amazing!" El Capitán says. "I feel amazing!"

"I know," Guillermo says. "I have regained my youth's strength."

"The Glowing Globe said—"Javier says.

"Stop!" Darkened Moon exclaims to keep him from talking, "That revelation is only for those who heard it. Guardians and Protectors must keep their destiny to their self."

"Okay," El Capitán says, "Gracias for your much needed consejo, amigo."

"Now let's go. We must get back to the village before the moon appears and rules the clear skies."

"I am content that 1 did not follow my first mind, Amigo." Cristobal says to Crissino as they walk back to the Seminole village.

"Why is that, Cristobal?"

"1 wanted nothing to do with this adventure, now I am grateful.''

"I as well, I did question my decision when the Admiral showed up. But…"

"Boom! Boom!"

"Bang! Bang!"

"What was that?!" Rogelio asks.

At a distance, near the village's direction, a small trail of dark smoke rises up.

"The village!" Darkened Moon says as he looks toward that direction.

Without any hesitation the entire expedition run towards the village. El Capitán and his men draw their swords when they get closer. He hands Catalina a sword as well in case there is a real emergency on their hands.

When they get to the village, there are pirates pillaging and slaughtering the people. The Seminoles left behind to defend it are making a valiant effort, but it's to no avail, devastation and the loss of life runs through their village.

Darkened Moon leads the charge to take back his village and those that remain alive.

"Caribs!" Kike exclaims as he spears an enemy.

El Capitán and Catalina fight side by side while they push the pirates back into defensive mode. Javier and Rogelio fire their weapons into the backs of Carib warriors before they are able to kill the young Seminole boys who found the courage to fight back.

El Capitán and Catalina end up splitting up as the battle gets more fierce. Catalina helps the young mothers get to safety with their infants and makes a path with her great swordsmanship. Just at the edge of the village, a pirate and the Chief of the Caribs reveal themselves behind a tee-pee hut. They stand in Catalina's way but allow the women behind her to escape.

"Arrrhh," he says, "She's the one, Piko, Take her!"

"I beg to differ," Catalina says as she artfully swings her sword and strikes the Carib and cuts a piece of flesh.

"A stubborn one she is!"

The pirate swings his blade and Catalina blocks it, but the fierce strength of the pirate brings her down to her knees. She defends herself from the pirate's advances, but each swing discourages her confidence and she realizes that his power is overmatching her speed and decisive quickness.

The reinforcements provided by El Capitán and his men prove to be too much by the intruders and they retreat.

"Alejandro!" Catalina exclaims. "Help!"

"Catalina!" he says as he turns around and tries to follow her cry.

"Help me, Alejandro!"

The pirate has a sword to Catalina's neck while he exposes his stance to let El Capitán know that he means business.

"El Tiburón!" he says while he thinks twice to charge him.

"Ahh-Ahh-Ahh-Ahh." El Tiburón says, "Do not take one step, Capitán De Los Amantes, or she dies."

"You coward! Fight me like a man, you pero del mar!" He spews out in anger with saliva, "I will kill you!"

"Ha! Ha! Ha! You fool, I cannot die Capitán!"

"You will, and it will be by this mano you Puerco!"

"Do it!"

He tries to step forward, but Javier tackles him as a stick of dynamite flies their way.

"Boom!"

El Tiburón escapes with Catalina and he flees back to the ship he commandeered from The Protectors.

"Boom! Boom! Boom!" goes off around the village and a fire

Alex Negrón

engulfs them from the exploding dynamite.

The canoes in the narrow river are also set ablaze to help El Tiburón make an unchallenged escape. El Capitán sees Darkened Moon holding his only son in his arms while tears flow from his face freely.

"I am so sorry." El Capitán says. "But we must go, he has my wife."

Darkened Moon raises himself up and wipes the tears that are drowning his cheeks and says, "Get her back, and avenge my son's death for me, Capitán."

"You have my word, Darkened Moon," says El Capitán, as he affirms his oath with a stiff handshake to reassure his new ally that he means what he says.

"Swift Foot will show you the way back to your ship."

Swift Foot raises his hand and shows them the way back. They hop through the blazing fire and they run to help rescue Catalina.

"I know where he's going, Capitán!"

"Where to, Ronaldo?!"

"He's going to the Bahamas, the Caribs have a hideout there!"

"Do you know the way?"

"Si, Capitán, I do! But we must hurry! We don't have much time."

After having to go the long way to their ship, it takes them almost an hour to get to it. They each hurry to get "El Amante Del mar" in sailing order to rescue Catalina. El Capitán, Ronaldo, and Javier head into his cabin to strategize cutting off El Tiburón.

"He most likely docked here," he replies as he points towards the tiny bay southeast of the river that leads to the Everglades, "and he's headed here."

"Don't worry, Capitán, we will get her back." Javier says to help reassure him.

"She's with child, Javier!"

"What did you say, Capitán?" Ronaldo asks.

"She's carrying my child…"

"Then we must really be expedient! He's going to try and open the sea's secret portal!"

"What do you mean, Ronaldo?' Javier asks.

"I once heard the Carib Chief and El Tiburón discuss finding the Incan treasure he lost during a shipwreck. He's opening the sea's portal by having a life within a life as the key to it."

"You heard the man," El Capitán says, "Let's get going!"

After twenty hours of constant navigation. El Tiburón's ship is just two clicks away from El Capitán's grasp. What was once a fancy and glorious ship that belonged to the Protectors of the Seven Seas, is now covered in black tar, with the front of the ship painted like the face of a shark with devastating sharp teeth to intimidate those that cross their path. The dreadful ship has a flag with a symbol of a vicious great white shark to signify that it belongs to thieving pirates.

"There he is," Eduardo says as he sits in the watchtower, "it appears as if he's waiting for something."

"Perhaps, it is us," El Capitán says, "Javier!"

"Yes, Capitán!"

"Prepare the men for battle!"

"Ay-Ay, Capitán!"

"Let's go full steam ahead, Rogelio!"

"As you command, mi Capitán!"

On the ship of El Tiburón, the pirates scramble when they see their foe break through the horizon and disrupt their evil plot to become rich, sailing mercenaries.

"I told you he'll find me!" Catalina says as she tries her best to loosen the ropes that have her tied to one of the ship's poles.

"Silence!" he says as he orders his men to be ready for the oncoming assault.

"He's going to kill you!"

"Arrrrh." he growls at her while he gives her an up close stare. "I said silence! I finally found the heroic Spaniard's weakness, and now I can finally defeat that thorn in my side and dwell in peace, arrrh!"

El Tiburón's face is very hard to bear. Being nicknamed, "The Shark", came about when an Incan spear split the left side of his face and left a scar near his eye. To embellish his name, he filed down each tooth very sharply, and it gave him the appearance of an old-seasoned shark that's been swirling in the ocean for decades with an unwillingness to perish. El Tiburón has been sailing the seas for over sixty years, and he's seen heroes come and go. But El Capitán is the only opponent that stirs his emotions up in a very hateful manner. El Capitán seems to be there to thwart his plans every time. Now, the tables are finally turned.

"Piko, begin the enchantment!"

The Carib Chief, Piko, calls out a spell towards the sky and black clouds begin to block out the sun's inviting rays. Thunder pounds while the clouds wrestle each other for superiority as the lightning darts across the sky while the rain pours out in buckets.

"What, in el nombre de Jesus, is going on?!" Guillermo asks as he stares at the blackened sky in a perplexed look.

"Are the cannons ready?" El Capitán asks.

"As ready as they'll ever be." Javier replies while the thunder continues to pound out.

The ocean's waves get higher and more violent as the unexpected storm intensifies. The waves make it harder for the men to reach the pirates and so Rogelio steers the ship right to give the Twins a clear path to fire at their ship with the cannons.

The storm kicks up hurricane winds and the waves circle around El Tiburón's ship to cause it to swirl around.

"They're getting away, Capitán!" Ronaldo exclaims.

"Fire the cannons!" El Capitán orders out loud.

"Fire the cannons!" Javier exclaims to relay the message.

"Boom! Boom! Boom!"

A lightning bolt hits the ship's top deck simultaneously and it causes them all to scatter to keep from being struck by it. When they rise up, the storm vanishes just as quickly as it has arrived. El Capitán raises himself up and he notices that the ship is gone. He scatters back and forth on the ship's top deck in complete dumbfoundness as he exclaims, "Where did they go?! How could they just vanish in a blink of an eye?! Someone please answer me!"

The crew is just as shocked as well, all but James and Kike.

"You!" El Capitán says as he points towards Kike. He steps towards him and grabs him in an aggressive manner and asks, "Where did they go?!'"

"Mundo Desconocido," he replies.

"Mundo que?"

"It is a world unknown, my dear amigo," James says, "Kike knows another way to get there."

"Where is this other way?" Javier asks.

"We must head to the island of Puerto Rico to find the entrance."

"You heard Señor James, to the Isla Del Encanto!" El Capitán Exclaims.

"We must hurry, time is against us!" Ronaldo exclaims.

The men quietly do their task and they set out to sea to help El Capitán rescue Catalina. They must find a way to get to her and defeat El Tiburón once and for all.

Mundo Desconocido (World Unknown)

In the midst of El Yunque's Rainforest, lies an entrance to a world that is unknown. A world that the Tainos have made their own. Join the Spanish Captain on this magical quest into El Mundo Desconocido. It is here, that El Capitán is willing to surrender all the riches that one's hands could ever possess and fulfill his heart's only dire request...

El Capitán sulks in his cabin. Tears flow down his cheeks as he sits in a lonely bed. The scent that Catalina left behind is not making the situation any better. The rest of the men think it's best to leave him be until they reach the island. The only one who doesn't have the sense to let El Capitán be is Kike. He feels that he should do his best to try to explain his side of the story and decides to knock on the door to get permission to enter.

"Leave me alone!"

Kike disregards his command and enters with a platter of food specially prepared by Edwin to help cheer their captain up.

"I said…" El Capitán says as he turns around to see who's the one that is crazy enough to interrupt his pity party, "What do you want!?"

"Capitán must eat, Capitán needs his strength."

"Leave it there and leave, Kike."

"I know you blame Kike, but Kike has no fault."

"You know the prophecy of the flames that Darkened Moon spoke about, am I correcto, Kike?"

"Kike knew in part, Capitán," he replies as he gets a little more comfortable.

"Please, Kike, tell me the story of your gente."

"Spaniards got attacked by Caribs who dressed and played like Tainos. Caribs and Tainos are mortal enemigos. Spaniards retaliate and kill Mucho Tainos. Kike's familia suffered death. Chief of Tainos found magic cave and cave save Tainos from extinction."

"Why didn't you enter the cave?"

Kike takes some time to reflect on his past and replies, "Kike lose mind, go very loco like pajaro and sought revenge. The Protectors help save Kike and Kike find new purpose, Capitán. New purpose for living. Darkened Moon reveal prophecy to me and said that I will live long enough to see Tainos return home. He say Kike will follow a rebel Spaniard into Mundo Desconcido. Darkened Moon did not reveal to Kike that Capitán goes to follow his Corazón."

"I believe you, Kike. How long have your gente been in this Mundo Desconocido?"

"Many moons have come and gone since Kike has seen his people enter magical cave. Now, Capitán must eat, we have a great journey to save Catalina."

El Capitán takes Kike's advice and pulls himself together. He finds the strength to face his worst fear since he has left España, and that's losing Catalina for good this time. He unrolls his navigational map and he strategizes a safe approach to Puerto Rico. He's certain that the word has spread about the charges he faces back home and he has to tread lightly when he hits any territory that belongs to his unrighteous King.

El Capitán orders Rogelio to navigate the ship to a very small island just south of Puerto Rico. When Alejandro first joined the navy, Admiral Rodriguez led them to this island to apprehend pirates that were causing problems in the Caribbean. Rogelio steers into the tiny cove, and all the men can tell that the hideout has been abandoned for years. In the mountain, there's a nicely cut-out tunnel that allows their ship to sail in and Guillermo drops the anchor to stop it from crashing into the back of the tunnel.

"What is this place, Capitán?" James asks.

"This is a hideout for pirates," Guillermo replies, "It took us years to find them. They hid right under our nose and this is why."

Guillermo points upwards and shows him a pulley system that is holding a curtain. They exit the ship with their supplies and load up their rowboats to prepare their trip to the main island. El Capitán pulls the rope and it releases the curtain. The curtain becomes the tunnel's camouflage and it assimilates as if its part of the mountain's side.

"Do you see?" Guillermo asks.

"It looks very realistic," James replies.

The island is just three miles away from the coast of Ponce, Puerto Rico. It takes them about an hour to roll their boats to reach the island shore. Kike takes the lead and he leads them through a very old and beaten Taino path when they reach the shore.

"Coqui, coqui, coqui, coqui, coqui.''

"What's that sound?" Crissino asks.

"Coqui, coqui, coqui," continues to take over the airwaves as the indigenous frogs chirp all through the island.

"Those Coqui frogs," Kike replies, "Coqui frogs are friends of Tainos."

The tiny amphibious creatures hop off the leaves and surround Kike. They jump for joy and celebrate the appearance of a long, lost ally.

"Coqui, coqui, coqui, coqui,"

"Why do they sound like crickets and not frogs?" Crissino asks.

"These special Boriken frogs, they call out the name of my great ancestor, Coqui."

"Why?" Javier asks.

"The mighty Taino King, Coqui, was the first man to step on this island many hundreds of years ago. King Coqui freed all the animals from the evil Levikato. A hairy serpent with teeth made of iron arrows and eyes that burn like fire."

"The Chupacabra?" Guillermo asks.

"Yes," Kike replies, "Levikato sucked the blood of goats and put all the animals into slavery. King Coqui slayed the evil, hairy serpent and the Boriken frogs call out his name in remembrance of the King's good deed.''

"Coqui, coqui, coqui," The frogs continue to jump and chirp in a harmonious rhythm while they continue to trek the path.

"Is this the way?" El Capitán asks Kike.

"The Taino caves are this way, Coqui frogs will show us the way to the magical cave."

They continue to hike north towards the Yunque rainforest when the clouds float over them when the day is just about to end. The clouds darken and release the buckets of water that they hold. The men hurry when they spot two huts made of straw just off the beaten path.

The cold drops of tropic rain has them shivering as they stay in the huts hoping for the rain to pass by. Instead, the storm intensifies and the frogs swarm around the huts while it does.

"Coqui, coqui, coqui. coqui."

"We will rest here for the night," Kike says.

"We must move forward," El Capitán says.

"Storm sounds angry, we rest here and find caves tomorrow, Capitán."

El Capitán unrolls his blanket in disappointment, he wants to press on, but he comes to his senses and lays down on the ground while the chirping hypnotizes his soul.

"Coqui, coqui, coqui."

The soothing chirps speak to his Spanish heartbeat and it causes him to relax for the time being. Each chirp makes El Capitán's eyes heavier and gives him the chance to take a much needed rest.

***

El Capitán opens his eyes and he feels rejuvenated as he wakes his men up.

"Levanta te hombres! Glory awaits us!"

"How much further, Kike?" James asks.

"We reach Cuervas before moon appears."

The men each get up and they have a little snack to eat before they continue on their journey. The frogs continue to be their guides through the tough jungle terrain. Ten hours into their journey is when they reach the outskirts of El Yunque's rainforest. Kike makes a quick stop when his instincts tell him that someone is very near when the sound of a branch snapping echoes in his ear.

Soldiers are patrolling the area and El Capitán's nerves race through his body because he knows that word has to be out that he is a wanted man back home.

"Jose!" a soldier exclaims.

"Que paso?" another asks.

"I see something by the old Taino path!"

"Run!" El Capitán exclaims.

"Bang!"

"Bang!"

The soldiers fire their muskets towards them when they see the leaves rustle while the men try to lose them in the rainforest.

"Bang! Bang! Bang!"

"Ahhh!" Pablo yells out loud when he hits the ground after being shot.

The Twins, Tuyen, and Pho help Pablo up and they carry him on their shoulders.

"Bang! Bang!" sounds off as James and Ronaldo fire back.

"Go! Go! Go!" El Capitán says while he makes the decision to help ward off the soldiers.

Pho hands him four sticks of dynamite to help buy them some more time.

"Bang! Bang! Bang!"

The torrid gunfire causes El Capitán, Ronaldo, James, and Javier to seek refuge behind some of the thicker trees. El Capitán tosses two sticks to Javier while Ronaldo and James fire their muskets again.

"Bang! Bang! Bang!" The soldiers return fire, and then there's a brief moment of silence.

"My name is General Ruperto Nunez-Rojas. Surrender or suffer muerte!"

"Desculpa General. I am Capitán De Los Amantes and surrendering is not part of my character! I beg you to please stay back— I do not wish any harm to you or your loyal men!"

"You are wanted by our King for many seditious charges. Please come peaceably. Out of respect for your glorious deeds, your men can go freely."

"I can't do that, General!"

"You leave me no choice, Capitán!"

He gives Javier the signal and they light up the sticks of dynamite and toss them at the same time. The General grants his men permission to fire again. Some of the bullets fly past them, while the rest blow chunks of bark off the trees they hide from.

A loud "Boom!" echoes in the jungle with patches of dirt and green vegetation flies upward with soldiers jumping out of the way. The four then make their run to catch up with the rest of the men.

As they get closer to the secret caves, another storm develops and the wind picks up in very harsh gusts.

"Is Pablo okay?" El Capitán asks between breaths.

"He was hit bad, but he'll make it." Guillermo replies as he applies pressure to the wound on his lower back.

They continue to march on and they get led to a large pond by the frogs that are still guiding them. A waterfall beautifully cascades over the mountainside's cliff and it gently crashes into the pond.

The storm gets stronger and it flexes its muscle to the inhabitants of the island to indicate that it's a hurricane.

"We are here, Capitán," Kike yells to cut through the howling winds as he points at the waterfall.

The population of frogs gets larger and they hop in and out of the pond, "Bang! Bang! bang!" goes off as the soldiers continue on with their pursuit.

"We must go now!"

They climb up the cliff while thousands of frogs hop up with them and show them an entrance behind the cascading waterfall. They all manage to enter the cave without any soldiers seeing them. Cristobal and Crissino each light up kerosene lamps while they hold it near

Pablo's back so Guillermo can stitch him up.

"Ahhh!" he exclaims as Kike pours rum on the wounds.

"Be quiet, Pablo!" Guillermo says. "I'm trying to concentrate!"

"Be fuerte, Pablo," El Capitán says as he firmly holds his hand.

"Ahhhh!." he yells as Guillermo digs the tiny projectile out of his wound.

Kike pours some more rum on as Edwin does the stitching.

"You see," Guillermo says as he wipes the blood on his hands with a handkerchief. "He'll live."

"Thank you old friend."

"De nada, Pablo."

"Guys," Cristobal says, "look at these paredes."

Loud thunder rocks the island's foundation while lightning spreads throughout the blackened sky.

"What is it?" El Capitán asks as he walks towards Cristobal and Otavio.

They show him the distinct paintings they see and they can easily tell that a story is being told on the cave's walls.

"Coqui, Coqui, Coqui, Coqui!"

The frogs hop in excitement, as the clouds get louder and louder from bumping into each other, the storm continues to lord itself over the island.

"What is happening?" Guillermo asks.

"They show us the way," Kike replies.

They follow the frogs into the heart of the mountain and they go deeper into the hollowed-out cave.

"This monte," Kike says, "is made from magical rocks given to us by the Cosmos. Water from clouds brings this monte to life and it opens its mouth to take us to the Mundo that is Desconocido."

At the end of the cave, there is a bright, neon green pool that is being filled by the water pouring out of the mountain's age-old cracks. The men are speechless as they watch Kike walk up to the pool and swirl it with his right hand.

"Coqui, Coqui, take me to the place I want to be," is the chant he speaks to open the secret portal.

The pool comes to life and it swirls on its own in a clock-wise motion. Everyone else steps back when the pool picks up in a rotation. A group of frogs hop in without any hesitation.

"General! General!" a soldier exclaims, "There's a cuerva here! I see a light and some shadows."

"We don't have much time!" Ronaldo says before he fires his weapon.

"Bang!"

A Coqui frog stands in front of El Capitán and chirps at him before he hops into the pool.

"We must go now before the storm passes!" Kike says as he helps Pablo jump in.

Rogelio and Eduardo each fire their weapons before they hop into the pool. Guillermo, Crissino, and Cristobal follow them; James, Javier, and Ronaldo hop in as well. Alberto holds onto Pajaro when he dives in head first with Otavio next to him. The Chinamen Twins hop in after Edwin while the soldiers storm the cave.

El Capitán is the last one left and he hops in when the soldiers fire away towards the back of the cave. The pool stops glowing and the storm vanishes while the soldiers stand in the cave in a bewildered manner. They had El Capitán trapped with no way of escaping, yet he manages to escape Spain's grasp once again.

They all slide down a magical water chute and they all manage to yell out in excitement while they wait to get to the other side.

"Coqui, coqui, coqui, coqui!"

The frogs hop on El Capitán and his men to use them to surf their way into Mundo Desconocido. El Capitán chuckles as a few of the legs tickle his exposed chest. He stretches out his hand and causes the glowing water to splash his cousin's face. Some of the water shoots into Otavio's mouth and it causes him to choke a bit on it.

"Ha! Ha!" El Capitán laughs while he points at him.

The crazy water ride comes to an end as each one dives into a pond simultaneously and they form a mega splash. They all come up for air with smiles on their faces. While they wipe off the excess water from it, a very large parrot is shielding itself from the man-made tidal wave. When it realizes that the splash is over, it spreads its wings and flaps them towards them to dry them off.

"That is quite a big pajaro," Guillermo says as all their eyes become fixated on the creature.

"Wahhh," Pajaro says as it flies towards his larger contemporary, "Are you papa pajaro?"

"Wahhh," The bird squawks out loud and continues to flap its wings dry.

The enormous parrot is five times the size of pajaro with extravagant fluorescent colors to coat his gentle feathers. The lime green feathers with a bright red to coat the tips gives awe to his admirers.

El Capitán approaches the creature with caution and the parrot squawks as it steps back.

"Suave, Suave, I will not harm you."

"Wahh, why are you here?"

"It speaks better than any pajaro I know," Eduardo says.

"And it's a whole lot sober than ours," Cristobal says.

"My name is Capitán Alejandro De los Amantes. These are my men, and we are protectors of the Siete Mars."

"Wahh, you're a Spaniard! Wahh, no Spaniards are allowed! Wahh, Spaniards destroy everything!"

"No, no, no," Kike says as he waves his hands while stepping forward, "They are with me. I am Kike, Son of King Sapo, and a descendant of the mighty King Coqui."

"Wahhh, Taino are friends! Wahh, Taino are friends," the parrot says, "Wahh, I Huraca. Wahhh, welcome to Mundo Desconocido!"

He turns about and he squawks out loud to get another bird's attention. The very large trees shake from side to side and a parrot larger than Huraca reveals himself to El Capitán and his men.

"That is a mammoth of a pajaro," Otavio says as he gazes awkwardly while the bird gracefully lands next to Huraca. Tuyen and Pho slowly nod their heads and say, "Very big bird."

"Hola, my name is Kako. Welcome to El Mundo Desconocido. Are you hungry?"

"How is it that you speak so well?" Javier asks.

"We call this place Huracán Island. A very strong hurricane swept this island and every animal that survived was able to speak as humans do. Would you like some canepas to replenish yourselves before we leave?"

"Canepas?" Rogelio asks.

"Canepas are very citrusy and sweet. They have the taste of mangoes and limes," Kike replies.

"We have plenty of fruit," Kako says as he motions for Huraca to retrieve the fruit, "the Tainos brought many delicious fruits with them, canepas is one of them, compadres.

"Where are these Tainos, my feathered friend?" El Capitán asks.

"Taino village is north from here. We must travel past these green hills and get to the Rio Coco."

Huraca drops large canepas into the hands of each sailor two at a time. The freshly-picked fruit is very round with a hard rind with the feel of a lime or lemon. The inside is a pulp that has a bitter-sweet taste around a marble-like pit. Normally, the fruit is the size of a gumball. But in this unknown world, it is the size of a softball. So are the mangoes, bananas and pineapples that spread around the green hills that have Pajaro Lake surrounded. Everything grows larger because the ground is very rich in nutrients.

The men still stare at the larger parrot Kako, while they suck on the fruit's pulp. He spreads his wings and his stance can make any of the earth's largest eagles feel inferior. Kako sports a coat of fluorescent blue feathers that looks as if they were momentarily dipped in Incan gold. His deep blue eyes give the reflection to onlookers that the Atlantic is in its winter phase of the year. A streak of blood red wraps around his beak to intimidate those whose intentions are meant for evil.

"Are you and your men ready to go, Capitán?"

"Yes, please show us the way, my feathered compadre," he replies.

Kako and Huraca spread their wings and flap them so they can take flight and show them the way to Taino village. The men can't help but take in the spectacular scenic view. The sun seems to be moving towards the east and its rays glimmer and shine brighter than the sun on Earth.

The small birds fly behind Kako and Huraca while they take the path that takes them to the north end of the island. Javier takes a deep breath and exhales as he continues to walk beside Alejandro. A feeling of ease and calm resonate with him as he soaks in the tranquility of this secret world.

"This is the place, Capitán," he says.

"What do you mean, Amigo?"

"This has to be El Jardin de Eden. This is the place my alma has been searching for my entire life."

"I sense the very same thing, mi amigo."

Just before they reach the river crossing to get to the village, four Taino warriors jump out and create a blockade with growling black jaguars. They threaten them with wooden spears with sharpened rocks at their tips.

Kike is the first to step forward to secure the safety of both parties.

"Wait! Wait!" he says with his hands up, "I Kike, son of King Sapo!"

One of the Tainos steps forward and orders the other three to step back and get the jaguars to calm down.

"I Tato, son of King Papote, and great-grandson of King Sapo."

Tato hugs his great uncle and tells his companions who Kike is.

They all embrace their long lost tribal member and kiss him with joy.

"Welcome, this is Bobo, Pito and Poo-poo. we guard the village. Father will be happy to see you; he has waited many lunas for the prophecy to finally take place."

They cross Rio Coco and walk through the village while the villagers curiously follow and whisper as they make their way to the village's meeting place. In the center, the Taino King is in his handcrafted prominent chair that is made out of bamboo and decorated with gold trinkets and colorful feathers. The guards that are tasked to stay by the King's side at all times take an aggressive stance and point their spears at the arrivals to get them to halt. The King stands up and he signals them to take ease. He can't believe who stands before his very eyes after so many years has come and gone. He has grown old, but his own uncle still carries the same face he had when they fled their homes.

"Tio Kike?!" he exclaims, "How could this be? How have you not aged?!" he asks as he embraces him with the grip of never wanting to let go.

"Kike drink from the Fountain of Youth. These are my friends," he says as he motions for El Capitán to step forward, ''Kike's friends are here to help."

Everyone bows to show the Taino King their respect. El Capitán steps forward and motions his hand for permission to speak. The crowd speaks out in clusters when they see that Kike's guests are Spaniards.

"Hush!" the King says, "What is it Spaniard?"

"I need your help, my wife was taken by an evil pirate named El Tiburón and he brought her into this mundo."

"Ooooh!" the crowd exclaims.

King Papote raises his hand to get them to be silent and asks, "Did you say El Tiburón?"

"Si," he replies.

"El Tiburón is a long time enemigo of Tainos, he seeks a treasure and he plotted against our people to attain it. He used Caribs to attack Spaniards while dressed like Tainos. El Tiburón is the razón we hid in this Mundo Desconocido from Spaniards."

"What treasure?" Kike asks.

Papote leads them to a nearby cave that is guarded by two Tainos. Kike, James, Javier and El Capitán follow them while the rest stay put.

"This is the Cuerva of Prophecia," he says as he grabs a torch.

The cave has writings and paintings on each side of the wall. They are very similar to the cave that allowed them to enter this distinct world. Kike reads each pictograph and sighs in pain when he recognizes whose symbols they belong to.

"When Tainos first entered Mundo Desconocido, a Taino dwelt in this cave. He went loco and began to paint these walls.

"He said that these visions came to him in a dream and swore to us that his lost son will come with a rebel Spaniard. This Spaniard will betray his people and come to Mundo Desconocido for matters of el corazón. He will need our help, and in return, he will bring us to our home in the known world."

They get to the end of the cave and on the ground are four treasure chests lying on the floor. He opens each one and El Capitán gasps for air as they gaze upon the chests' contents.

"This cannot be," El Capitán says, "It's the Treasure of the Royal Serpent."

"The elders considered my grandfather insane and disregarded his claims. We have been waiting a lifetime for his prophecy to be fulfilled."

"Didn't Guillermo say that the treasure rests at the bottom of the Atlantic abyss?" Javier asks as he runs his hands through the golden items that is in the third chest.

"My grandfather recovered this treasure near the western coast of the island. El Tiburón's ship had been sunken by a fierce hurricane. He hid the gold in the cave that the Coquis show him."

"We need to find him, will you help us?" El Capitán asks.

"There's a ship that is wrecked in the cove where the bitter and sweet water meet. Perhaps, you and your men can repair it and sail to an isla north of here. This isla belongs to the evil Caribs, they call it, El Isla De Muerte. If El Tiburón is here, he dwells on that island."

"Show us the way, King Papote."

"I must stay and prepare the village to defend itself. My son, Tato, will show you the way."

El Capitán quickly leaves the cave with Javier, Kike, and James and gathers the rest of the men.

"Tato," he says.

"Si, Capitán."

"Show us this wrecked ship."

"It is near Bitter-sweet cove, the river will lead us there."

"Will you also help us get to this Carib isle?"

"That is a very dangerous island, Capitán."

"Your father believes El Tiburón is on that isla."

"Then I will show you all," he says and then he calls out his companions, "Bobo, Pito, Tito, Poopoo, Keko, and Siko come with us!"

Huraca, Kako, and Pajaro soar the sky while the men travel along the river. The river's gentle down-stream current seems as if tiny diamonds are being carried along for the ride while they journey north. The three birds display their graceful flying by swooping up and down and skimming the top of the river. Huraco controls his body and dips his right wing into the river and splashes Pajaro.

Pajaro shakes off the splash and lands on Huraca to take a brief rest to survey the island's beautiful landscape. Two of the jaguars playfully jump on each other and wrestle along the riverbank. Playing begins to get serious as one ends up in the river and wants to pay the other back with a swift right paw to the face.

"Chiro, Charro, stop it right now!" Tato exclaims.

"But he started it, Prince Tato," the one on the left says.

"The large gatos speak as well?" Pablo asks as he limps along.

"Animales or hombres," Capitán says, "We do not fight amongst each other, my feline compadres."

"Please forgive us, Capitán, it will not happen again." Charro says as he lowers his head.

"We are very close, we must get around that monte," Tato says while he points towards the mountain to indicate how much further they have to get-to the wrecked ship.

The crew takes a brief moment to drink from the river.

"Ahh," El Capitán says as he parches his thirst with the cool water. This water is very sweet," Cristobal says. "Sweet, like the water of Cocos."

The path leads them around the mountain to the island's cove. A large waterfall spills over a cliff with sparkling water into the cove's pond. On the right is a sandy beach made of seashells that has been crushed by the tide for centuries. The tide calmly rolls in and gently kisses the island's coast every five or so seconds. The birds fly around the cove while the men and jaguars each take a deep breath of admiration as they stand high on a cliff next to the waterfall. To the left lies a large warship that is perfectly framed as the mist of the splashing water latches on its side.

Large bright and colorful trout sprout in and out of the water. The cove's scenery is like no other, it's as if God himself made it to be his own personal fishing hole. Nowhere on earth can these brushstrokes of beauty can ever be mimicked or imitated.

They make their way towards the ship and the rest of the men notice that James has an extra pep in every step he makes towards it.

"This can't be," he says as he moves faster.

"What is it?" Javier asks as he tries to maintain James' pace.

"I know this ship," he says as he checks to see if it truly is the ship.

They get to the back end of the ship and the faded gold lettering reads:

"The Atlantic Glory"

"My father was aboard this ship."

"Are you serious, Señor James?" Rogelio asks.

"It is twice the size of our vessel." Guillermo says as he analyzes it's actual girth.

"This was built in the Shipyard of Baltimore, Maryland. It was the most splendid vessel to be built by the colonists in honor of the King. It made a voyage to Jamaica and never returned. Only one survivor was able to tell this story that no one believed. It drove him mad and he uttered ridiculous sayings. He said that a massive storm caused the mouth of the sea to open and it swallowed the ship whole. He said it was between Florida and Bermuda."

"And you say your father was aboard this ship?" El Capitán asks.

"He was the Captain. He proudly served Britain twenty years before the ship disappeared when I was only a lad."

"How long ago was that?" Ronaldo asks.

"Thirty years ago," he replies.

"It seems empty," says Javier as he gazes upwards.

"Huraca, Kako, find the ship's boarding plank and secure the deck."

"As you command, Capitán," Kako says.

"Wahh, secure the deck."

"Capitán," Javier says, "Take a look. Here's the ship's breech."

On the ship's right side, the boards are chipped and cracked, the damage looks as if it scraped alongside something jagged.

"What do you think caused it?" Guillermo asks.

"Over there," Javier replies as he points towards the sea.

On the side of the cove's entrance are two massive rocks with sharp edges. Pieces of the ship's debris still lingers as if the rock on the left took a bite of it.

The two birds work together to get the plank in position to help the others board the ship.

"Let's get to work, we must get the ship up and running before nightfall." El Capitán commands.

James is the first to walk up the plank and heads straight for the captain's quarters. The rest of the men awkwardly stand on deck and wait to see what James finds.

El Capitán walks in and he hears his English friend crying very lowly.

"Señor James," he says as he cautiously tiptoes his way towards him.

At the navigational desk sits a dead corpse with a pistol still held in his left hand. It hangs barely above the wooded floor while the body slouches over the desk.

"How could this be?!" comes out of James' mouth as he wails over his father's dead body.

"Now, now, Amigo, it'll be okay."

El Capitán is trying his best to console him, but he's speechless at the time. He looks down towards the desk and he sees a blood-soaked note underneath the corpse's forehead that's pressed against it.

"What's this?" he asks.

James finds a moment to swallow the tears and leans his father back on the chair. The blood-soaked note says:

"Beware of the Sea of Calamity"

In one of the cabinet's slots, a large parchment that is rolled protrudes out of it and it gets both of their attention. Some of the blood splatter caught its edges and El Capitán reaches for it. He unrolls it to unveil the parchment's contents and a map of this magical world gets revealed. Just to the north, and slightly to the left of Huracán Island, he sees an island shaped like a broken dagger and the name of it is titled "Isla De Muerte".

"Can you find his log, Señor James?"

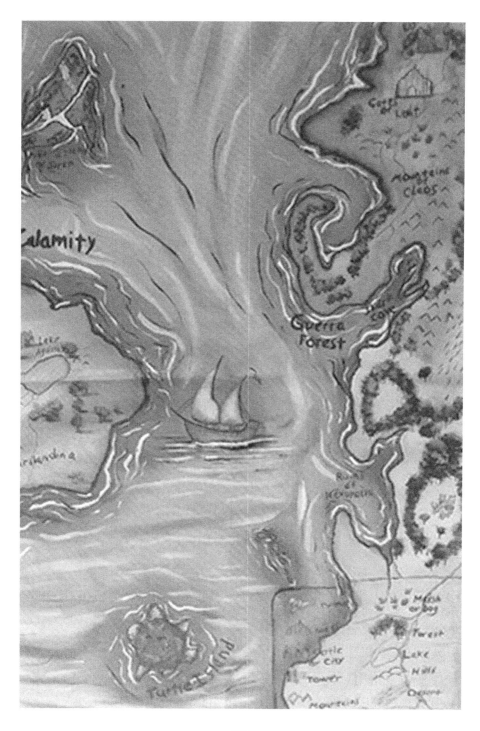

"It's right here," he replies as he checks his father's personal items tucked into the main drawer, "He's spent many years navigating this land, his logs can help us. Here's where El Tiburón is located. That's an oddly shaped island, Capitán, and it's a lot of ground to cover."

"Not if we start here, Señor James."

He points to a place that is titled, Skull Mountain, and its location at the top end of the dagger's handle near the bay.

"I'm sorry for your loss, Señor James."

"Gracias, Capitán, but now is not the time for mourning. We have a lot of work to do."

They both step out and El Capitán looks everyone in their eyes, "Tato, I want you and your men to retrieve us some of those splendid Pescaos that begs us to eat them."

"Si Capitán," he replies.

"Guillermo, Edwin, Eduardo, Crissino, and Cristobal, find the tools and fix the breech."

"As you command."

"The rest of you, get the ship in sailing conditions and make planks to rock the ship off the bed it's sitting on."

"What about me, Capitán?" Pablo asks.

"Read this log and see if there's anything useful. Señor James and I will give his padre a proper burial, make sure you bring us some shovels."

"As you command, Capitán," Pablo replies.

About half the time it takes to dig the hole for Captain Charles Galumbo's resting place gets spent in silence. The only thing heard in the background are the echoes of the birds, and the water colliding in the pool to go along with the sound the shovels make with every scoop of dirt that gets tossed.

"So tell me, what's your story?" El Capitán asks, "I'd hate to be ill- mannered and assume."

"Never mind it, Capitán."

"Do you want to know my historia?"

"We have time, sure why not."

"My father is a butcher and being the heir of a butcher was not on Catalina's father's wish list for the qualifications to be his son-in-law. We were going to run away, but he discovered our plans and had me beaten like scrambled huervos."

"So what did you do?"

"I joined the Navy and I sought the glory and fame that comes with being the best sailor. I knew being a butcher would never allow me such fortune. It broke my father's heart to see his own seed reject the trade he was proud to possess."

"Wow," he says as they keep shoveling, "I could never get my father to be proud. He would mock me and call me a spoiled bugger who was unfit to carry on the Galumbo namesake."

"Muy harsh."

"You're telling me, Capitán. I joined the Protectors to prove him wrong, but when I returned home, he was gone."

"I'm sure he'd be proud of you now, Señor James."

"Probably not, but there goes the saying, 'you can't pick your parents'."

139

"Very wise proverb, amigo."

They lay the captain to rest and cover up the shallow hole. James says a brief prayer on his father's behalf and they both close it with the sign of the Cross.

"Capitán! Capitán!'' Pablo exclaims as he and Javier approach them.

"What is it, Pablo?"

"Ahhh!" Pablo says as he grimaces from the still very fresh gunshot wound. "I found something here."

"What does it say?"

"Capitán Galumbo talks about this strange island that is shaped like a dagger that belongs to savage inhabitants. The island's plant life is all dead and has the color of grey ashes. The island sucks life dry and it grants anyone any desire he seeks if he sacrifices the life within a life of one of his enemies on the darkest day of the calendar."

"Catalina, she's with child, that's what life within a life means!"

"That's not all, the Tainos say that the darkest day of the calendar falls tomorrow on the new moon, they call it, 'Dia De Los Muertos'."

Alejandro's heart drops down to his abdomen when he hears the bad news. El Tiburón plans to sacrifice Catalina to retrieve the lost treasure he stole from the Incans. Javier signals for the other two to leave them alone so that he can speak to El Capitán privately.

"Are you worried?"

"I can't lose her again, Javier."

"Since the moment we became amigos, you have only managed to fail at two things."

"What is that?"

"You go out of your way to die the most thrilling way possible and yet you stare at the Angel of death in his eyes and mock him every time."

"What is your point, Javier?" he asks while he sticks his shovel into the dirt.

"Your integrity is above any man I know, including my own. You're supposed to let me do the worrying while you attain us the glory."

"Gracias, Javier. So what's my second failure?"

"You always fail to match my comely beauty," he replies as he slaps his back with a couple of chuckles.

"This integrity you speak of must be very high."

"Higher than the ship's mast."

"How do you manage to secure that tiny hat on that grande cabeza?"

"With coconut oil," he replies and then says, "Now let's go and save your esposa, she carries my nephew. Let's just pray he receives Catalina's looks."

"How do you know it's a boy?"

"I will not have it any other way. Someone needs to inherit these deceptive tricks I have up my sleeve."

***

The crew manages to get the ship fixed and out into the open sea. As they sail towards El Isla De Muerte, the boat now boasts a new name as "El Protectador" gets seen from behind in big black letters.

The Great Britain flag that waved so proudly on the ship's mast is now replaced with a flag bearing a Coqui frog as their emblem and insignia. El Capitán stands at the forefront of the ship impatiently waiting for land to be seen. They had spent the whole night sailing, now that half the day has expired, darkness chokes the sun with black clouds and billows of smoke. Thunder echoes across the land as they see land up ahead.

"It was just very bright," Javier says as he looks towards the sky.

"This place is very evil," Tato says as his friends nod in unison to agree with him.

They get to about three miles south of the island and the three birds fly away to scout and seek out the enemies' whereabouts. As they wait for the three parrots to return, the smell of sulfur invades their nostrils while the clouds continue to get darker and darker.

Huraca, Kako, and Pajaro come back about forty-five minutes later. Kako lands on deck while the other two hang on top of the ship's sailing masts.

"They are here, Capitán," Huraca says as he shakes his head to get rid of some of the ashes that fell on his head. "They are exactly where you suspected they might be. They are camped at the foot of the skull-shaped monte. She is being held in the skull's left eye."

"And El Tiburón?"

"He is with her, and I have to say Capitán, this is one very ugly pirate. He bears a large scar across his face near his right eye."

"That scar was given to him by a fierce Incan warrior. His spear nearly killed El Tiburón near the mountains of Peru." Guillermo says.

El Isla De Muerte is a very strange place. It exists only through death, the leaves are very dry and gray as if the life of all the plants have been drained. Just a single touch to anything and it easily crumbles. The dark powers that have taken root on this island seem to be devouring the life forms that exist on it.

While the men make their way to save Catalina from the evil El tiburón, the camp at Skull Mountain is getting prepared for the sacrifice. Drums are being struck and the Caribs are dancing in a circle with loud chants being yelled out in their native tongue.

Catalina is in the mountain's eye and tied to the wall. She constantly wrestles with the rope to try to free herself, but the effort just leaves her wrist with a nasty burning sensation.

"Arrrrh," the old pirate says, "There's no escape, my dear. That's one thing I can assure you."

She spits in his face and says, "You embece! You will die in the hands of Alejandro!"

He calmly wipes the spit off his face and then he seizes her face in wrath and reveals his sharpened teeth to show his displeasure.

"The only thing your Alejandro can do is watch you die!"

She tries to shake his fierce grip by jerking her head from side to side and he lets her go.

"But don't worry, Catalina. You and your child will not die in vain! Once I satisfy this island's thirst for innocent blood, it will grant me all that I desire!"

"Not if the Protectors stop you," she replies.

"Silence!" he says as he gets in position to backhand her. "Neither they or anyone can deny me this desire!"

El Capitán puts his men in the perfect position to attack the enemy's camp. He sent Tato and his men to secretly swim towards their ship to sink it. He orders the two parrots to create a decoy to allow him to climb the mountain unnoticed. And when the timing is right, he will order his men to fight El Tiburón's evil crew.

143

"I should go with you, Capitán," Javier says before they break the huddle.

"I want you to lead our men. This thing between El Tiburón and I is now personal and long-awaited, my good friend."

"Very well," he says, "I guess the only thing left to say is, To Glory!"

He pats Javier on the back before he motions for them to get into position. He then slowly and carefully finds his way to Catalina by climbing up the mountain. Huraca and Kako distract the Caribs by dropping dried up coconuts on their camp while they dance around.

A Carib tosses a spear and Huraca's superb aerial skill gives him the edge in dodging it. The spear almost hits El Tiburón and he exclaims, "Watch where you are throwing your spears! Arrrrh!"

The Carib Chief keeps himself in the moment as he continues to chant out loud with his arms aimed towards the sky. The clouds get more violent with thunderous claps to synchronize with the Carib's drums.

The island shakes while El Capitán tries his best to keep from falling off the steep cliff of the mountain. The skull's mouth erupts with blood spilling out as it drenches the chanting Carib and his expression shows that he is relishing in the moment.

El Capitán finally gets to the skull's left eye and he barges in with a heroic entrance.

"Arrrrh," growls out El Tiburón while he squares off to fight by drawing out his sword, "How did you find us?!"

"For a seasoned Pirata, intelligence is not one of your strongest traits. Hand her over and I will spare your wretched life!"

"Arrrrh. I will never do such a thing, Capitán!"

El Capitán refuses to spare anymore pleasantries and charges the ugly pirate to begin the battle. The aggressive charge takes El Tiburón by surprise and puts him in a defensive stance as he meets El Capitán's blade with his.

"Get him, Alejandro!"' Catalina yells as she still tries to jerk herself free.

"No te precupe, mi amor," he says between swipes, "Soon, this'll all be over."

He kicks El Tiburón in the shin and then takes him down with a swift sweep to the legs. He jumps on top of him to finish him off, but El Tiburón Defends himself with his two feet and pushes him backwards to force El Capitán to land on his back. The Caribs see a commotion taking place and another spear finds its way and nearly catches El Tiburón again.

"What did I say about those spears?!"

El Tiburón becomes the aggressor and he swings his blade while El Capitán tries to get back on his feet.

"Alejandro!" Catalina exclaims as she briefly closes her eyes.

El Capitán manages to hold his sword up and escape a mortal blow to the clavicle. He punches the wicked pirate in the gut and causes him to stumble backwards momentarily. He reaches for his pistol and signals for the men to make their move as he exclaims, "Ahorra!" while he fires his weapon.

Javier and the men on land attack the Caribs before they try to help their leader that's above them. Huraca and Kako swoop in and drop boulders on them as well. Pajaro flies into a Carib's face and pecks at it.

As the Carib screams and tries to protect his eyes, Pajaro says, "Wahh, give me rum! Wahhh, give me rum!"

A large "boom!" sounds off as two cannons roar from El Tiburón's ship. The Tainos led by Tato quickly jump out before the cannonballs that were fired straight up rips the ship and sinks it.

"Arrrrh, you bastard of a child!" El Tiburón furiously says, "Now you owe me two ships!"

He charges again and El Capitán maneuvers himself to the side as Kako flies into El Tiburón's chest. The collision knocks the pirate out and it leaves him unconscious. El Capitán immediately rushes towards Catalina and unloosens her from the ropes. She plants ten kisses on his face before he's able to do so.

"I knew it! I knew it! I knew it! I knew you would find me!"

"I missed you very dearly, mi amor! Come on let's go."

"Wait, wait. How did you do it?"

'It's a long story, now let's go," he says as he pulls her with him, "Oh, you forgot this."

He hands her the sword she left behind at the Seminole village. They leave out of the skull's left eye and make their way down the mountain, while the fight below them gets heated. Tato and his men swim to shore and join the battle as well.

Javier is fighting with every inch of strength he has as he takes on two Caribs at a time and overmatches them. A Carib tries to sneak up and cut off his head with a machete, but Eduardo fires his gun and catches the Carib in the back. Javier turns to process what just took place and gives Eduardo a nod that indicates that he is indebted to his patron.

A spear catches Eduardo in his right leg and goes through the thigh with the tip protruding through the front.

"Ahhh," he cries out as the pain shoots through his body while he hits the ground.

"Bang!"

Javier runs towards Eduardo after he shoots the Carib that tossed the spear fifteen feet away.

"Are you okay!?"

"There's been better dias, Compadre."

"Come on, let s get you out of here. Huraca, help me out!"

"Wahh, wahhh, wahhh."

Huraca lands by them and Javier helps Eduardo get on top of the parrot.

"Take him to the ship and have Pablo tend to his wounds."

"Wahh, as you command, Wahhh!"

El Capitán watches Huraca take Eduardo away when they get to the foot of the mountain. On his way down as well, is El Tiburón in a hurried pace.

"You will not get away this time, Capitán!"

Crissino and Cristobal try to double team him, El Tiburón outwits them and badly wounds the both of them with cuts to the chest and arm respectively.

"Capitán!" he yells out loud to indicate who he wants next.

The Carib Chief and another Carib stand beside El Tiburón while he drenches himself in the bloody waterfall. Javier and Ronaldo stand next to their captain and they make their way towards their opposition.

Once they get close enough, El Capitán hops in midair and swings his sword simultaneously to press El Tiburón back. Their swords clang once again as they both get the feeling that only one is going to walk away from this fight once and for all. El Tiburón thwarts each swing and tactical move that Alejandro has in his arsenal. Catalina comes from out of nowhere and makes it difficult to be on the offense. He swoops in and dodges her assault and pushes her away.

"Arrrhh, this false honor you display is your weakness and will be your ultimate demise, Capitán."

"Loyalty and honor is the only way my heart will beat on, Tiburón!"

El Tiburón makes his move and brings the fighting to them as he wields two swords to take them on. He manages to slice El Capitán's abdomen and wounds him badly. El Capitán holds his wound while defending himself. Catalina catches a slice across her arm and drops her sword. El Tiburón kicks it away, and then strikes another blow to El Capitán's thigh and discards his sword as well.

"Arrrhh," he says as he's about to deal Alejandro with a final blow, "The day has finally manifested itself and my most desired dream has come to life."

Just before he deals his strike, Catalina scoops up her sword and tosses it near El Capitán's vicinity. Javier and Ronaldo take out their foes and watch what takes place before them. El Capitán rolls to his right, snatches the sword, and pierces El Tiburón's chest in one swift motion. The unexpected move shocks El Tiburón as he drops his sword while he dies slowly.

Catalina limps over and towers over him to watch his bitter and cold soul wither away. El Capitán stands next to her and kisses the top of her head.

"Your dream has now become a deadly nightmare," he says as he holds onto Catalina.

El Tiburón's eyes slowly roll back while his life fades to black. The rest of the surviving Caribs surrender when they see they are overmatched by the fearless Protectors of the Seven Seas.

The blood that is being spewed out of the skull's mouth dries up. The dark clouds dissipate and allow the moon's light to shine across the night sky. The men are battered and bruised, but they muster the strength to celebrate their victory.

"Wahh, it's over," Pajaro squawks out loud, "Wahh, let's drink rum!"

El Capitán gets assisted by Catalina and Javier as they volunteer their shoulders to help him get back to their vessel. A sigh of relief flows through the entire crew and a calm sense of peace comes over them.

"Do you feel that, Compadres?" Rogelio the Moor asks.

"Feel what?" Tuyen asks.

"Freedom, mi amigos. We are finally free from the King, his Prince, El Tiburón, and pirates like him," he replies.

"Amen to that," James says.

"To Glory!" El Capitán manages to say between grimaces while Catalina attends to his wounds.

"Viva El Mar!" They all exclaim.

"Capitán," Otavio says.

"Si, my young prirno."

"What do we do now?"

"We fulfill our destiny and prophecy, and lead the Tainos back to their home!"

To Be Continued...

149

About The Author

Alex Negrón was born on January 17, 1981 in the city of Chicago. He grew up in the Humboldt Park and Logan Square area. You can also find his contributing works on www.PrisonLectionary.net and poetry on www.minutesbeforesix.com. Alex Negrón is a passionate voice against any and all modes of systemic oppression and a champion of the arts of humanity.

Made in the USA
Monee, IL
12 February 2020